Prologue the War

During a great war between the forces of heaven and hell, a group of scientists invented a device, to harness the energies of angels' the gadget was to be the first-ever time machine, to stop the devastation which befell the earth. The experiment was to no avail because the motor malfunctioned and then the engine exploded.

Many miles above the Lab, an Archangel and a Nephilim were in battle. The archangel's bodily physique was well-toned, and her muscles structure was what any bodybuilder would be trying to achieve. Her wings and hair were silver; She also had the most beautiful radiant yellow aura which encompassed her entire being. She wore the most splendid armour that had a pure fluorescent white glow which covered her from head to toe.

She had her sword the ready to strike down a Nephilim. Upon the archangel's blade, there were seven multi-coloured jewels, each of the gems represented one of the seven main archangels who opposed Satan. Every gemstone had a remnant of power from an angel which shared their properties. The pattern engraved upon the hilt of the sword was very cool. A blue flame enveloped the blade. Every angel wielded the holy sword of the spirit, and it splintered throughout the cosmos. The sacred essence of God imbued it with the fire. Which shared the quality with the holy spirit which allowed it to be in multiple places at once

The Nephilim was very ugly too look upon; its eyes were black with toxic green bile oozing out of them. Its skin was red and flaky; the creature had four spikes upon its head and three horns. The wings upon this monstrosity were ragged, neglected, and ugly. It had paws which resembled the claws of an eagle, wrapped around a black flaming sword.

"This is your end Seraquin!" screeched the Nephilim whose blood-stained wings were dripping, Seraquin flew into battle chanting an angelic battle cry "For Michael!" she yelled. The motion of her wings was majestic and beautiful. She knew there was no way; heaven was going to win after the loss of the commander, so she loosened his jewel from the hilt of her blade, which was a blue gemstone.

The Nephilim swung his sword, but Seraquin parried his brutal attack. A flash of white light sparked as the blades clashed. A baby blue jewel detached from the clanking of the swords, Causing the gemstone to hurtle towards the earth and the explosion.

The explosion was not like that of a standard blast, for the detonation was the manifestation divine energy of heavenly forces whose grace was unquenchable; therefore, the flames were not able to be quelled by any earthly manner. The jewel took the brunt of the blast from the bursts of energy created by the explosion, and it drew the divine source of energy into itself, thus stopping it before it became any worse. A detonation of this calibre would last for an eternity eradicating anything in its paths. The gemstone fell amongst the rubble, and it glowed an array of different colours.

Meanwhile, there was a young man called Darcia, and he had a scar above his left eye and many bruises caused by the skirmishes he had faced. His hair was bright red, curly, and bushy. His eyes were opal and equipped on his body was armour which had a blue Glow and a sword that had the same ambience. He was scrawny, but you could tell he could hold his own in a fight How else could he of survived the conflict between heaven and hell, which had been raging from long before he was born. He was seventeen, and his life had not been easy. Most of his life, he had been fighting monsters who had been ravishing the world feeding upon human suffering. Unfortunately, angels could not protect everyone because they could not be everywhere at once. Darcia had a small pouch upon his hip which carried all his Gadgets.

He was in a battle with a creature known as Asmodeus. Asmodeus turned out to be an unholy and despicable beast. Who caused a woman called Sarah to suffer in her love life by killing any male she laid with *forcing her to be alone until God sent Raphael to work on his behalf who gave Tobias instructions to save Sarah*

Fortunately, God sent an angel to free her of this curse. The angel brought a young boy named Tobias to her aid and gave him instructions on how to purge Asmodeus from her life. When the deed was complete, he asked for her hand in marriage.

Asmodeus had the appearance of green gunge like creature; he fed upon the unhappiness of the human soul. The beast would do whatever it took strip a soul of its joyfulness. It was not as easy for a demon to seize a person's hope as it was in the times of the old. Humanity was now able to see these dark entities. Through a retinal device implanted from a young age, the design was by a scientist called doctor frank Linford.

He had created it during a time of great distress frank started to hear voices. During the 21st century, he was diagnosed with mental health issues, but this was not the case; his soul was more attuned to hearing what others could not. He knew something was off with his medical diagnosis. Luckily enough, he was smarter the average joe. Thus, he designed the occulai devonium, which allowed him to see a world outside of his own. His work was not complete for being able to perceive the demons was not enough he wanted that which ailed him to be purged from his life, therefore, with the help of angels he created the sword of Zathor and armour which limited the power of demons.

All his idea's kept Darcia alive and gave him the power to fight the unseen. Through the story of Sarah and Tobias Darcia knew how to make Asmodeus retreat; the study of the bible was mandatory when you were fighting demons. Burning a carp's heart, but that was not a viable answer for Asmodeus would only be able to cause more people to suffer in his wake, he had to put the demon out of its misery.

As Asmodeus was on the ropes pleading for his life, Darcia heard squawking, which could only mean one thing. A flock of hellish birds were closing in. at this, the only real solution was to withdraw himself from the conflict. There was no way, he was going to retreat, without first finishing off Asmodeus, he raised his sword and impaled the evil sprite. As his weapon pierced Asmodeus, it glowed, and the fiend exploded toxic green bile which smelt putrid and was extremely dangerous.

The breastplate Darcia was wearing had exceptional capabilities for moments just like this, and it manifested with a force field which repelled the bile, keeping Darcia out of harm's way. He knew he had to flee before the possessed animal appeared. If he stayed to fight it would have been game over. Demon bird's eyes were very adept at homing in on their prey. If you are in these birds' line of vision, you were more likely to die.

The birds would have overrun Darcia. So, he jolted, trying to find the nearest Portpad. The rebellion positioned Portpads all around the earth, and each one teleported you to a base of the uprising. Darcia could not count the number of times when portpads had saved his life, getting him out of a dire situation when he needed to escape the most. Portpads were another one of franks great inventions.

As he was running, he tripped over rubble; he was where the lab once stood. Darcia automatically put his hands out to cushion his fall; at this moment, his life flashed before his eyes. He thought this fall would be how it all ended, and fortunately for him, he put his arms out to shield his fall and landed upon the angelic gemstone then it embedded itself into his skin, Darcia didn't feel a thing.

He heard the squawking getting closer and closer until it was too close for comfort he twisted his body to look behind him, and what he saw was the crows big red, dark luminous eyes gazing into his own they were less than a two metres away he closed his eyes. Then panicked saying "it is over it is over." The terror he felt activated a power in the jewel light came from his hand and enveloped him.

For a few minutes, he trembled not noticing the light had saved him, the jewel had transported from a catastrophic moment to a world he had never known. He realised he had not been torn to shreds and touched his body to double-check, and then Darcia opened his eye. The young man was astonished by what he saw.

The whole world seemed to have incomparable beauty in comparison to his reality. Buildings were undamaged, and he noticed small robotic machine speeding by at 40 miles per hour; this was the first time he had ever seen a moving vehicle.

He found joy at seeing how everyone seemed happy and carefree, not fearful of what may be lurking around the corner; this place was nothing like the war.

Suddenly, he heard a man "spare change." he begged, the man was in ragged ripped clothing and looked scruffy he had an odour which offended Darcia's nostrils. Beside the man was a small hat which contained copper circular things Darcia could not recognise.

Darcia had no clue what the man was on about considering money became obsolete. The way you obtained things in his time was by trading whatever you scavenged when you were out. Also, homeless people did not exist because everyone was practical without a home. Staying in one spot practically put a target on your head, and you were likely to lose your life. Darcia knew this all too well, staying in one place made him lose his mother

Chapter 1 Darcia's horror cavalry against the tainted

For a second Darcia looked all around him admiring the things people took for granted, he looked up at the sky, which was not red, but grey clouds were gathering. Everything was peaceful; he never felt this safe in his entire life.

Birds were chirping, which was an unfamiliar sound. He averted his gaze to find out what was making the sound. As he was turned a building caught his eye. with the words Tesco illuminated above the entrance, with green neon lights, a young boy stepped through an automatic door which bedazzled Darcia he had never seen such a contraption.

The Boy was five foot nine, which was rather tall for a boy of his age. He had golden-brown pupils and was a rather chubby child. His hair had been dyed blue which was his favourite colour, his natural hair colour was red, and you could see that from the freckles upon his face he had plump chubby cheeks. Older people had the urge to pinch them; he did not have any appreciation for this attention because sometimes it hurt. His left ear was pierced but not by choice; his mother got them punctured at a young age; he was too young to remember. The boy was wearing a camouflaged tracksuit and had a backpack that matched his outfit; he had a crucifix upon his neck. Upon his skin, there was a tattoo a washable tattoo which came in a packet of candy cigarettes.

The same man who asked Darcia for change asked the boy "spare change." The boy rummaged through his pocket and generously dropped his last bit of change into the man's hat he had three pounds, and even though other people told him it would only go on drugs, he felt it was better to try and help and fail than not to try at all.

The man seemed grateful for the money the boy had contributed. Some days he hardly got any help people just walked by turning a blind eye to a man whose pocket was bare. He thanked the boy for he would be able to eat that evening. Then he lay down upon the hard-concrete floor, covered himself with a filthy sheet and closed his eyes. the floor was cold, but the man had become accustomed to the hard-cold gravel where he lay.

The boy felt happy from his good deed. He decided to head home when, suddenly, he noticed Darcia. Whose outfit was peculiar, this piqued his interest he was intrigued by what Darcia wearing for he had never seen anybody dressed like that, nor had he seen a weapon such as a sword in Darcia arsenal. The sword had an ambience which was out of this world, and it glowed.

"Cool it's a knight." Said the boy, you could hear the sheer excitement in his voice. Then he reached out to touch the rim of the blade saying, "wow it glows." Darcia knew his sword was Dangerous and yelled "no don't touch it!" fear engulfed him he was scared the boy's life, for if he were not pure of heart, he would have experienced instant vaporization. At the same time as yelling, he tried to parry the boy's hand away. But it was a little too late the boy's fingertip was upon the blade before he knew it Darcia failed to stop him. The sword did not do any significant damage because the boy was untainted enough not to be eradicated. It did manage to graze his skin though, but only because Darcia had startled him when he shouted. Darcia was glad the boy was stood before him and not reduced to a pile of cinder. Frank Linford designed Darcia's breastplate with the capability to act as a conduit, so he was protected from the effects of the weapon

The boy was unharmed and did not understand the implications of his actions, nor did he see the danger. Darcia scolded him "stupid boy you could be dead!" the boy was confused he was also astonished, the idea that their possibility of death from a mere touch Made this weapon seem like the most potent weapon in the world.

Darcia decided it was far too dangerous to leave his sword in a primary mode designed to strike down the impure fiends of hell. The sword had different elemental abilities dependant on which type of spawn of hell you faced. So, he pressed a button upon the sword which went white with bolts of black electricity flowing across the blade. Then he pushed it again, the colour of the edge also changed too red, and it had a flame resonating on the blade. He pressed the button a final time; the weapon became a standard sword. His sword had eight modes. But the sixth mode was best to fight Asmodeus.

The boy's jaw dropped he had never seen anything like it or at least not in the real world, the boy was in shock he found it hard to talk "w w w where di di di did you get that?" he asked the boy managed to compose himself mid-sentence. He was fascinated by what he had just seen it was unexpected.

The sword reminded him of his favourite video game samurai Sediko, so he stated "that sword is mystical! Just like samurai Sediko my favourite video game." A rush of excitement overwhelmed the boy Darcia did not understand what the boy was talking about then asked: "what exactly is a video game." Not knowing about games of this era it showed he did not have much of a childhood. The Boy never thought he would have to explain a video game how on earth does he not know. So, he described video games Darcia's face became more and more perplexed the more the boy said. So, the boy gave up on explanations and decided he would show him.

He introduced himself "My name is Michael, what is yours?" Michael then told Darcia "I will show you what a video game is if you want to see?" Darcia is my name." usually Darcia would feel an uneasiness diverging such classified information, for that was how the demons were able to take control. Something about Michael made him feel comfortable.

Michael started to wonder where this mysterious man came from; he pondered a few ideas. Maybe he is from my video game then he realised *how stupid that sounded, he thought for a second then the idea that this man was from the future entered his mind, his guess was entirely accurate.*

He wanted to find out a bit about the man and his arsenal of weapons he wondered what other types of cool trinkets he had. "if you don't mind me asking where you are from and how old are you, I am thirteen." Michael was a bit of a chatterbox and would talk your ear off given half the chance. it was apparent that Darcia was young Michael paused then exclaimed: "it is my birthday today."

Darcia could not remember the last time such trivial things concerned him, with heavens war raging there was no time to celebrate the day he was born. He never wished Michael a happy birthday but how was he supposed to know the customs of birthdays without first observing one himself. "London," he said, then explained the future. "in my." Michael interrupted abruptly. "London how do you not know about video games?" the boy was more puzzled at Darcia's reaction moments ago. not just by the fact that Darcia had not heard of a video game. Also, by the fact that weapons like this existed in London. If they did, he would have seen them during his school trip to Buckingham Palace.

Once again, Darcia started to explain "where I am from is nothing like here, we either flee or fight and scavenge to eat, heaven and hell are at war. Demons scour the earth in search of victims the year I come from is 2999 at the age of eight, a demon slaughtered my mother in front of me, and my older brother Jarion, by a demon called Abraxas. This moment influenced me to join the cavalry against the tainted."

Michael was shaking and interjected, "I am scared." The whole idea of wanting to see where Darcia came from was no longer an option. His face was pale like he had just seen a ghost then he continued "the year is only 2022, so I am safe aren't I" Darcia didn't feel right in telling how him the apocalypse started eight years from now. With the fall of the only angel who could close hells Gate when they opened. How could he the poor child was quaking in his boots? He knew in such a peaceful era of human existence; diverging the unpleasantness of the future would be terrifying especially for a child.

Darcia underwent fear for most of his life he was scared every day, understanding any day could be his last. He saw too many casualties too many fatalities on the battlefield from being underfoot of the scourge of hell, who would not be frightened. Death was prevalent in his life, and most soldiers hardly made it past 30.

Before Darcia joined the rebellion, he lived with his mother, who did what she could to shelter her boys from the outside world and the horror that lay in wait for them. His mother would often bless their house with holy water by dousing the four corners and doors and praying. Darcia could not remember his mother's prayer, but it seemed to keep them safe. Until the day his mother was unable to make it to the well of angels, the streets were too dangerous, the war was right outside their door. She saw demons ravishing human beings and knew if she left, she would not be able to keep her children safe the warding was failing.

She knew she had to get her children to a less hazardous environment, so she picked up Darcia and passed him too Jarion screaming "hide, hide!" you could hear the trepidation in her voice, but her life mattered less to her than her offspring. She gestured to a cupboard suddenly there was a big bang something was in the house with them.

Darcia and Jarion could see their mother through the little slits in the doorway. She went flying then they noticed her flesh flaking off but could not see her attacker, until the last moment when it finally finished tearing their mother apart. Darcia went to scream, but Jarion's hand was quick enough to snuff out the sound.

Every fibre in Darcia's body froze, neither of them was able to move. The demons continued to stalk the house in search of any survivor; it was like she was not its primary target. "Come out, little ones Abraxas won't hurt you." it sneered aggressively. Darcia's blood started to boil fear left his body, stupidly jumped out of the cupboard. Not thinking all he wanted was to destroy the demon. His eyes watered as he saw the pool of blood which surrounded his mother.

He lost focus on the demon which sprang towards him, Darcia and his brother lost all hope. A bright white light filled the room, and a cherub sliced demon in two from head to toe. within the illumination was an angel, with tears were welling from its eyes and rolling down its cheeks the angel's aura was white, and he introduced himself. "I am Raphael little ones I came to escort you to the rebellion."

Raphael knew God planned great things for Darcia's life but was not able to diverge such information; the worst part of it was Darcia would lose everyone he ever really cared about in a moment. After they arrived at the rebellion, Darcia made a vow that when he was strong enough, he would never hide again.

Darcia's memory was cut short by Michael, who said: "come on then." Gesturing for him to follow, which was probably a good thing PTSD kicking in from the memory of the awful ordeal.

Chapter 2 the power of the jewel awakens

On their journey, they walked through a park across the grass, which was rather tall, there was a beautiful array of flowerbeds, and a lovely aroma was coming from the flowers. There was a play area for children who were full of joy playing on all the apparatus within the park.

Then it started to rain luckily enough. Michael had an umbrella in his backpack; he used it to keep them both dry. Darcia had never seen an umbrella before if people were bothered by rain enough to use an umbrella, they would leave themselves open to attacks. Parents hurried to find shelter, and some picked up their children and went to leave the park in a hurry as to avoid getting wet.

They took about an hour to reach Michael's house using side alleys and every shortcut Michael knew. As they arrived, Michael became giddy as he revealed: "We are here." Like it was some great news. His house was an average semi-detached terrace with a blue door; it was a relatively small looking building.

Michael rummaged through his pockets to find his key and started to panic when the key was unfindable. He checked again by clearing the clutter from each of his pockets somehow during his first search the pass evaded him, so he knew a more in-depth investigation was vital, his he ruffled through his pockets which were full of paper. He searched thoroughly and found it in the first pocket he initially looked inside this happened quite frequently because he overfilled his pockets.

He unlocked the door then entered the house in as he stepped in through the door a golden retriever sprang towards him wagging its tail, and barking the dog was happy to see its owner. Darcia panicked, and he went to draw his sword in self-defence "hell hound." he roared.

He Forgot all demon-fighting features were off, Michael spotted him out of the corner of his eye and screamed "no he is friendly!" the dog jumped up with its hind legs on the ground and licked Michaels's face. Darcia thought Michael would have to fling it off and almost swung his blade to protect him, luckily enough for the dog Michaels words did not fall upon deaf ears.

This animal did not only have different attributes to a hell hound. Its whole persona was different from creatures in his time; it seemed friendly which baffled Darcia. Michael ordered the dog to get down, then said: "sit rover." When the Dog obeyed Darcia mouth flew open, then he asked, "How have you made a hell hound obedient?"

Michael scratched his head and said, "hell hound, what do you mean? he is my pet dog." Michael was puzzled by Darcia's question "wow I wish it was as easy where I come from, all animals are under the influence of demons we don't have pets."

He remembered reading about pets once but thought they were just legends because how could you tame such ferocious beasts. The image of a savage beast such as a hell hound tamed by people evaded his perception. It was hard to imagine something that was against humans in a good light.

As Darcia got fully through the entrance, the house was less compact then Darcia expected it to be. There was picture mounted on the wall which contained Michael and two other people. There was a small table with a device Darcia could not recognise it was a telephone.

The way Darcia contacted the rebellion was different inside his suit there a communication chip that which linked every soldier's uniforms together. If you needed to talk to someone, all you had to do was say their name two times, and the suits would link. The walls had a flower pattern; the carpet was red with white and gold spirals. There were stairs alongside the hallway.

a soft and gentlewomanly voice called out from a room along the hallway. "Michael, dear, are you okay? And how was your day at school?" the voice was southing to Darcia's ears. There were three doors along the walkway. The boys walked towards the voice, which came from the end of the hallway. Michael shouted "yes mum, I am okay. and my day was great," the closer the came to the entrance, the lower his tone became.

Michael opened the door saying ladies first in the same way he would joke with children from his school. Michael's mother was doing the dishes, putting knives and plates on a rack as she cleaned all Darcia could see was the back of her head and dark red hair. The kitchen was relatively small, and the flooring was laminated; the layout was what you would expect of a kitchen.

Michael became excitable when he started to explain how he met Darcia, his mother heard his story and put it down to an overactive imagination the sword part had to be.

She turned around to introduce herself she had flawless skin and blue eyes. her nose was rather long and pointed upon her neck was a tattoo of an angel, and she was wearing a green dress with a rather exciting design it had embodiments made of rhinestones. "I am Molly young man and Michael has done a good job of introducing you Darcia, nice to meet you."

Molly was rather pleased her son was making friends a few months ago she had to help him get out of a toxic relationship; his friend was a user. The person took advantage of Michael's kind nature; he knew Michael was willing to help anyone and took liberties. The usurper almost got him into trouble by influencing him in a way that only benefited himself.

Molly poured the boys a drink of fresh orange juice as she was passing them over the drinks, rover jumped up at Michael this made him accidentally drop his glass all over himself and the floor he tried to stop rover, but his command was too late.

He went to get the mop then wrung it out he started to clean the wet floor Darcia watched in amazement as the mop soaked up the orange juice spillage. There was no time to do little things like cleaning in his time. In a surprised voice, he bellowed "that thing absorbs liquids." With how many things Darcia did not understand made Michael question whether he was from the future or a parallel universe. Because if he were from a later time would he not know the purposes of a mop Darcia's world seemed like it had regressed.

The words he used activated the jewel within his hand fluids from every angle started gushing into his flesh. Everyone was scared, and Molly no longer questioned the authenticity of Michael story or believed it to be a figment of his imagination because now she could see the truth in it.

Michael asked Darcia to "stop?" but Darcia had no clue how and why this was happening. I cannot he replied a little bit scared of whatever was happening, Michael had a brainwave and told him to go to the hall to create distance between him and the liquid, when he was far enough away the liquid stopped flowing into his palm.

Michael followed him to the hall he was astonished by the power Darcia had just demonstrated. he wanted to know more about the future. He asked: "does everyone in the future have this ability or are you unique? this power is awesome." Darcia was as shocked as everyone else, he had never seen anything like it and to make things worse his hand was glowing, with how many gallons shot into his palm, he was scared his hand it was going to explode.

Molly was terrified and froze for a second; she did not understand what had just happened. she had never seen anything like it. She tried to tell him to get out, but her words were not working. The woman was in shock; questioning if it was an illusion that is it an illusion. She thought she became grounded because of that idea and her nerves calmed immensely.

She told Michael he would have to get his friend to leave, but Michael wanted to keep his promise. So, he begged his mother to let him stay. He threw a towel over Darcia's hand as to stop his mother from seeing that it was glowing as if she had not already seen enough to influence her answer into being a big fat no.

She did not know why she crumbled at seeing Michaels puppy dog eyes; she found it hard to deny him when this expression was on his face. Even though she saw what Darcia did and it scared the living daylight out of her, something inside of her told her to let him stay.

It was a rather calming voice; it sounded like her husband, who had died when Michael was five years of age. She could sense this boy was where he was supposed to be, and knew Michael needed some male bonding.

He always told her he wanted a brother and something about the boy seemed familiar. She answered, "Darcia can stay as long as you finish your homework!" Michael knew he had no homework so that meant he could bond with Darcia a whole heap more "I don't have any." He yelled.

Running up the stairs signalling Darcia to follow with a hand gesture, whilst shouting "thank you." to his mother.

The passageway upstairs had a different design there was no wallpaper the paint was a creamy colour the carpet was baby blue there were not many doors, and all were closed all except Michael's whose room was painted blue.

When they entered Michael's room, it was immaculately clean, Michael could not stand clutter, and if one of his toys were out of place, he would go into a frenzy. There were posters hung all around the room, and he had a small single bed and Mounted on the wall was a paper-thin television.

Michael wanted to know everything he could about the future, so he started hammering Darcia with questions, "can all people from the future do that? Or is it just you? What other cool things can you do? Is there any way you can teach me?" Darcia knew he had to say something or the questions would never end so he blurted out an answer "I couldn't teach you even if I wanted to, I have never seen anything like it, to be honest, I would have appreciated this if happened during the war."

His hand started to glow even brighter now; he just wanted to know how he could make it stop. He was frightened he needed his hand, and what if it suddenly combusted.

A farfetched idea came into Darcia's mind but what harm could it do try he decided to speak oppositely. too when water gushed into his hand and in the most simplistic way, he said: "send out as heavenly armour." At first, he planned to say water but something in him blurted out heavenly armour. A ray of beautiful golden light flowed from his hands amidst the glow they could both see armour materialising as like magic.

The light dimmed, and in the corner of the room where the light had shone there was a beautiful breastplate Michael's jaw dropped, and he squealed "wow!" the armour looked like Darcia's armour, but it had more of a radiant glow. There was one main difference near the shoulder blade; there were two slits as too not restrict an angel's wings.

Michael decided he was going to put it on; it was not that heavy it was made of supernatural material. Weirdly he felt acquainted with the armour, but why did he think this way? There was like a part of his identity was within the armour.

Darcia started to wonder what saved him from the crows was it the same thing that caused him to attract the water into himself if so could it be "no that's impossible it was only a myth" he thought out loud.

He remembered his mother used to repeat a prophecy as a bedtime. She told this story each night, his thought he could not be contained within his head "the prophecy could it be? No, no, there is no way! How could it be?" Michael overheard him rambling, but the armour entranced him, so he did not pry into whatever Darcia was saying. Eventually, Michael became tired of the armour and put it to one side

He started to think about the story his mother told him he remembered every detail. The prophecy engraved itself upon golden tablets which resembled the tablets that contained the ten commandments that Moses wrote. inscribed upon these tablets was something entirely different to laws of Moses instead the engravings were a message for the future. It said during man's darkest ages. A hero would arise. His one duty will be to protect and guide the archangel, as to change his fate, driving him away from the catastrophe that brought him to his knees. In a time, long before the war through the power of his angelic jewel, this hero will be able to manipulate matter, thus creating miracles, they are the wielder of the miracle jewel.

Chapter 3 Limuel Lingus

With this realization, he knew Michael's soul was not of earth, and it was his job to protect Michael no matter the cost. He could not allow his divine essence to ebbed through the darkness as it had been drained in Darcia's timeline, many years before Darcia was conceived, in an apocalyptic time. The enemy of man found a way siphon the energy of an archangel; this archangel was the head of the heavenly army. His power allowed them to open a gate to the underworld. Thus, demons had the upper hand; Darcia would not let history to repeat itself.

He wanted to fall to his knees and bow before Michael, but he knew angels far too well. Michael would not except exultation for this belonged to God and God alone. Even an angels' role was to glorify the Lord in all they do.

Darcia was awestruck by the fact that he Got to meet the archangel who was the biggest adversary of Satan. He knew he had to let him know his role, but how could he explain this to a child. He thought long and hard about the words he would use, but as he finally was about to speak up about who he was, everything started to spin.

Everything in the room except Michael and Darcia intermingled, which created a putrid colour, which was unearthly. There was also a smell of sulphur which caused Michael to become engulfed by fear," what is happening" Michael muttered under his voice.

Darcia had seen this once before and knew what was happening the experience was scary their essence was teleporting, to a place that was not good. Something from outside of their world was summoning them to its abode. "demons are warping us into purgatory," Darcia yelled.

A long time ago when Darcia was Michael's age a demon named Baal forced Darcia's essence into purgatory, at this age, Darcia had already joined the cavalry against the tainted or C.A.T.T. for in short. Purgatory was an awful place it was full of misery and unfulfillment; there was a thick mist which made it hard to breathe.

The fog distorted Darcia's vision, who became succumb with terror; every bone in his body had stiffened; he found it hard to move. He knew whatever had summoned him did not have a good cause. Throughout this experience, he could not calm his nerves. He remembered feeling an awful presence, and his nostrils were burning from a putrid smell. He saw people who were betwixt life and death suffering a restlessness from the pain of their demise.

The rebellion had given him a small black flare gun with the ability to Peirce the veil between worlds. The colour of the signal would indicate which world you were in so that your platoon could come to your aid and you would not be alone for too long.

The signal fire was picked up by a soldier whose name was Limuel Lingus who saw the smoke. which has a distinct colour of grey and had streaks of red flowing through the centre thus Lingus knew which world had trapped his comrade.

Limuel Lingus was small, small enough to be mistaken for a child. He had untamed blonde hair and a scar, which slanted diagonally across his blue eyes; he was well toned.

He was one of Darcia's favourite generals, Lingus had taken down many demon hives and most the time came back unscathed. On the odd occasion, he came back broken and bruised some times when he returned from a battle he was close to death's door but through it all, he always managed to come back with a smile on his face.

All the weapons carried by soldiers could pierce reality creating a rip, but it was a one-way trip. The only way back was to destroy the demon that drew the cadet into that reality. Lingus sliced through the air *making the tear through the fabric of reality into the depths of purgatory then he walked into the rift.*

Meanwhile, Darcia found a place to hide he heard a demon snarl "come out and bow before me, Baal likes it when you bow!" his voice sent shivers through every fibre of Darcia's soul. Baal was a construct made of stone, but you would not expect anything less from an idol. He was a manifestation created by the impurity of worshipping false gods. After the world tipped into chaos; a lot of people lost the moral compass, which led them to faith in falsehoods.

Darcia despised demons they were detestable and vile creatures, so there was no chance he was bowing to one. Yet he had no clue what his options were the beast roared "I smell your fear; it is only a matter of time before I find you." Darcia could not hide forever, and he knew that reinforcements were nowhere. So, he decided he would face the beast head-on, so he jumped out of his hiding place, ready to face the fend.

When out of the blue unexpectedly Darcia heard Lingus call out to him but this was a mistake and unfortunately so did Baal who lunged towards Lingus. Who was unaware of the incoming attack did not, and before he knew it, there was a claw in his chest and death was imminent?

This moment was Darcia's chance to launch a stealth attack; he crept up behind the monster withdrawing his blade as quietly as possible. Making sure his feet did not make a sound and his weapon was in a mode which could defeat Baal. He became more and more terrified with each passing step, he wanted to turn back and not face the creature, but he knew that would spell out his doom.

He had an adrenaline rush as he crept up on the monster then He raised his blade and stabbed the fiend in its back, but the edge did not go deep enough to kill Baal. The not, so fatal blow caused the monster to remove its claw from Lingus as to use it on Darcia.

Darcia thought it was over, but Limuel Lingus used his last bit of strength to plunge the blade deep into the heart of the beast. Then he fell to the ground the creature split into thousands of stone fragments.

Lingus knew he had to hold on for long enough to let Darcia know how to escape, so he fought death hanging on by a thread his life-force was ebbing. Knowing if he didn't, his death would be in vain as soon as Darcia saw dying and broke Down "no!" he cried "hang in there major. Limuel!" Limuel coughed blood and spoke, "my fight is over, reach into my satchel the lamb's blood burn." Then he gave up the ghost.

Darcia listened he was disheartened by having to see his favourite soldier die before his eyes. Baal was the first of many demons he had his hand in killing he burned the blood then he was transported back to earth.

During his time in the rebellion, he had learned a thing or two that would keep himself and Michael safe. His top priority protecting Michael there was no way he was going to allow himself to fail. The price of failure was too much to take

Chapter 4 He is an angel battle in purgatory

It was not long before they the demon had teleported them into purgatory, which had not changed; it was dark and eerie everything looked withered, purgatory had drawn life of the atmosphere. And with time it would also drain their life force. The only souls who had a chance of surviving a realm like this were demons or a soul which were devoid of purity.

Purgatory was a place that devoured the righteous soul-sapping away from the beauty within the flesh, causing those who traversed purgatory to become a husk a mere shell of what they once were. Darcia heard an awful screech which went through him he recognised the sound was that of possessed cats. These cats are known as hades super feline, and they sounded close, Darcia felt uneasiness, knowing such beasts were here. With the realization of what these beasts were capable of panic overcame him. One bite one scratch would cause the victim soul to leak into the underworld, and the wound was unlike an average cut that you were able cartelized because no bandage could keep your soul in your body, once they ripped your flesh it was game over.

He was not Going to risk losing the one hope for the future, so he yelled absorb Michael light encompassed the boy pulling him into hand until neither Michael nor the light was visible.

Darcia knew their arrival in purgatory was down to one or two things they were either summoned by Baal or Killias the king of demon wanted to gorge upon Michael's soul. Darcia heard a voice which sounded like thunder "do you think that will keep him safe, it only makes it easier to consume both your souls."

Darcia searched for the creature then heard a horrible cackle, but there was no sign of Killias. He knew the beast was in hiding, waiting for the right moment to strike. He recognised the danger at hand and reached for his sword then changed the mode to purge as to suit his environment. This transformation caused his weapon to have a glass-like appearance and gold rays of light flowed through it.

Darcia jolted in the hope to put distance between himself and the creatures that wanted to consume him. He came to an area which looked quite earthly; it was an alleyway. It was not a good idea of a place to retreat to, but there was no other path. It was like some outside force manipulated the reality. No matter which way was his chosen course, he kept coming back to the same place the alley. Which made his only option to face whatever lurked in wait.

As he got about halfway through the alley, he found himself surrounded by the Hades super felines. The cats had teeth that looked sharper then razor blades there was a green toxin oozing from their mouths', other than that they looked like normal cats.

It started to rain but not average earthly rain; the rain was blood. Darcia raised his weapon and got into a stance that showed was ready for battle then the cats lunged towards him.

The cats leapt simultaneously, something unexpected happened the sound of Michael's voice came out from Darcia's hand beckoning "Rover." In a loud, muffled voice. Then all of a sudden a golden light appeared and amid the light was Michael's Dog who no longer looked the same his fur was golden, unlike a dog's earthly form he had silver wings and a white aura surrounding him. He opened his mouth to bark and a divine wave of pure golden energy dispersed through the air eradicating each demonic cat in his path.

Darcia heard the distinct word "duck!" Within rover's bark. So, he heeded the warning he raised his sword above his head. The last of the cat plummeted through his sword, splitting the critter in two it fell to the floor becoming goo then it disappeared.

A glimpse of a mysterious shadow caught Darcia's attention; he knew this could only mean one thing, Killias, the king of shadows and bringer of darkness, was about to rear his ugly face.

Killias was a tadcoel which meant his speed was unfathomable and unrivalled. Which was evident by the cut that appeared on Darcia's cheek blood trickled down his face, but it was hard to see amidst the rain.

Most demons found great pleasure in inflicting pain before they murdered their victims. Demons downplayed their enemies, and this was their greatest downfall, mainly when they dealt with an experienced soldier like Darcia. He knew a thing or two about tadcoels and other demons; they were no different in purgatory than the ones he faced in battle.

He knew eye contact would give Killias control; all tadcoels can shatter a person will and turn them into mindless drones. Evading eye contact was the best way to deal with tadcoels. Darcia was ready for situations like this. He created an ointment made with two parts one part of the elixir was the blood of a tadcoel, and the second part ingredient was similar to what Tobias used to heal father's sight in the book of Torbit, the Gaul bladder of a carp. The fish for the ointment was a different fish; it was the kingfisher Brixham.

Darcia rubbed the ointment upon his eyes, knowing his sight was a necessity when fighting demons. Without being able to see Killias had the upper hand, he could not see because of the rain.

Killias had no nose, and his teeth were in the placement of his nose, they were onion-like with many layers filling his mouth, with teeth. His skin was black and covered with spikes; his eyes were translucent. He had many tentacles surrounding the majority of his body, upon his face, there were two black holes, at either side which were symmetrical, and one at the top inside a yellow triangle, his hand had four claws his legs were thin. His skin was an off yellowish colour with the odd brown patch.

Darcia knew the ointment had a time limit. So, he would have to dispense of Kilias as quickly as possible in the most time-efficient way. He fumbled through his satchel and pulled out a small golden orb.

The orb was a holy grenade filled with angelic grace, the explosion it caused was unlike to a standard grenade. When thrown it sucks the demon inside. Then utters the sacred word which only angels can speak. If this word were even to touch the lips of a human being, it would incinerate their essence. It had already brought Satan to his knee. The name held too much power for a fallen angel to take, without their grace, they were powerless.

Darcia knew Killias's speed would be a problem. He would have to find a way to slow the demon down substantially, or else Killias would flee, and the usage of the holy grenade would be ineffective and pointless.

So, he pressed the button on the hilt of his blade, which caused his sword to have the power of dimension piercing. He then started to draw an hourglass with his edge. He sliced the hourglass in the middle this cause a wave of sand to appear out of nowhere. There was a lot of sand; there was no way Killias could avoid it. The massive landslide was heading his way; his speed was now to the level of a mortal.

Darcia threw the grenade and Killias tried to flee, the grenade Emitted energy that caused Killias to be terrified. He did not realise his speed reduced until the moment he needed his speed the most. He wanted to be far away from the orb, but without his speed, Killias was a sitting duck. Before he knew it, the grenade vacuumed his essence then sacred words *pierced his ears, the name sounded like an explosion and lucky for Darcia could not make out the word. the colour of the explosive wave was multi-coloured.*

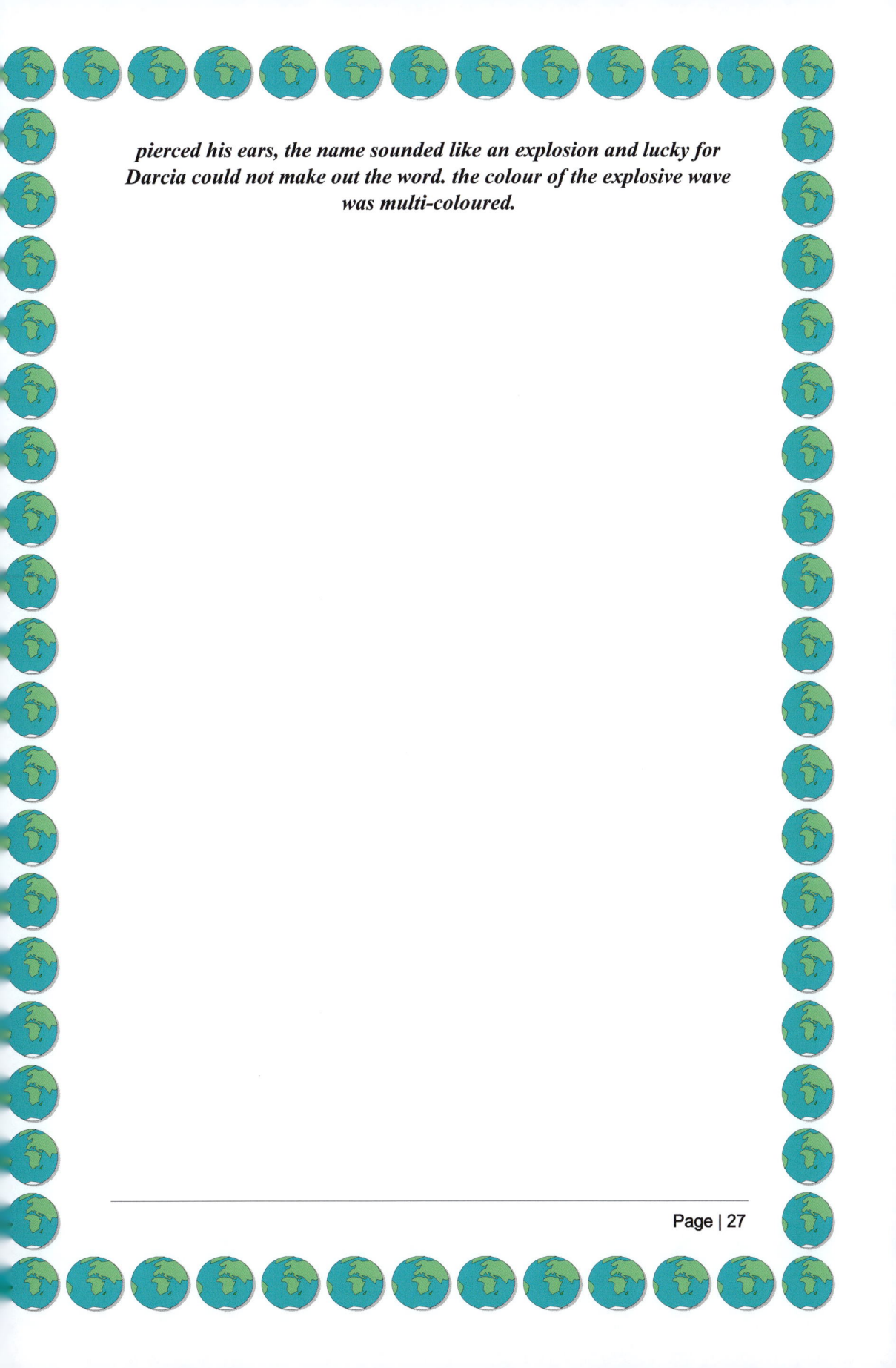

Chapter 5 Abaddon and the rebellion

A creature appeared which looked like an eagle the fur of a lion encompassed the animal's body. Furthermore, the animal had the paws of a bear. Darcia did not know if it was friend or foe, so he readied himself for a battle. Encase the creature attacked, but it did not strike. Instead, it spoke, "I am the first of the seven holy spirits who sit before the throne of God, I am here to assist the archangel Michael. Allow me to merge with his spirit before he arrives!" the last few words sounded urgent.

Darcia could sense the creature was on their side, so he yelled: "divert the energy of Michael as it was." He changed his wording not knowing if it would work the jewel still operated the same white light came out of his hand and amongst the beam, Michael materialised it was a quick process. As he had fully emerged the spirit stepped into his body, then his eyes rolled to the back of his head, and he fell he was in a trance.

Before Darcia had a chance to worry, he felt an unpleasant presence which seemed familiar, and it terrified him, he felt dizzy and weak. Then the world beneath Darcia's feet started to shake, and he could feel his molecules shifting this awakened a memory which had been buried by trauma. Abaddon was a demon which stole his brother's life, the one who the rebellion could not triumph over.

Abaddon stole so much away from him that day, his brother was the only family he had left was sent into a battle they could not win, to buy the rebellion some time. We all knew he was not coming back, and Darcia volunteered to take his place, but his brother would not allow let that happen, knowing this mission was likely to be his last.

He would not even accept Darcia help for he had no wish to see his brother martyr himself for the regiment, the whole squad felt the demon's dark influence. They knew their only option to banish the creature; was for somebody to be cannon fodder and Jarion drew the short straw.

His role was to distract the fiend; the commander handed out seven gate closing crystals to his infantry were given to the best soldiers of the garrison. Jarion had to distract the beast long enough for each member of the quadrant, to place the crystals around it; Jarion had a crystal and the most dangerous job.

As they arrived they came across the creature it was the size of an elephant, it had two black horns and flaming eyes, it was a three-dimensional shadow-like creature it had a silver tongue and razor-sharp claws so sharp the concrete beneath its feet split.

Five well-trained soldiers laid crystals around the beast with ease Jarion's distraction was going well, Darcia lost his stepping almost falling to the ground at this he alerted Abaddon's course who started galloping towards him. The truth is Darcia wanted the brutish ogre to notice him so that his brother could place his crystal safety, but Jarion threw his Chrystal to the side. There was no way he was going to let his brother die his protective brotherly instinct kicked in.

Darcia was about to place the Chrystal, but his brother's reaction threw him off, and the monster was closing in, its flaming eyes etched themselves into Darcia's nightmares. Jarion saw his brother in danger and acted irrationally; he put his life on the line because his brother was important to him more important than the mission. If only he had seen this fall as an opportunity, the result would have been different, and he jumped in the way of Abaddon's claw as it swung at Darcia it was suicide yet it was for a good cause Abaddon's claws ripped right through him.

The commander placed Jarion's crystal, Darcia was not going to let his brother's death be in vain, and he set the last Chrystal around Abaddon. This warped Abaddon from the battlefield with Jarion still connected to its claw. Darcia was traumatised by this mental image throughout his entire life he blamed himself.

He knew neither himself nor Michael was ready to face off against such a demon, especially one with that much power. Looking at the Michael condition, there was no way he would be able to fight. Darcia burned the lamb's blood, knowing this was the only way to escape this reality and the pull of Abaddon. For this domain was a territory which Abaddon held power over. He put his hand upon Michael just before the teleportation began and in seconds, they were no longer in purgatory now they were back in Michael's room.

Michael became placid as soon as they returned to the real world, he also became furious at Darcia and growled. "why did you absorb me I could have fought too!" this reaction took Darcia by surprise. Yet, he understood the urge to fight and knew the side-lines were never attractive, especially when you have the spirit of a warrior.

Darcia did not want to take any unnecessary risks. He knew Michael was too crucial, so he took the time to explain his role "I had to when I realised who you were, your safety became my top priority. You are the archangel Michael, every 400 years a seraph is born. This seraph is the saint of that era. All angels must undergo the trials of mortal life. Usually, the role of the angel is to subjugate a sin from the world, and in doing so, they sanctify the world claiming sainthood. You are the leader of Gods heavenly army and one of the angels which oppose Satan. Your role is vital you put monsters beneath the feet of men, that they do not transgress. In my world, Satan defeated you, without your command, the heavenly hosts became out of touch with their unit in the field, which gave demons an upper hand. Many were overwhelmed; thus, without you, leading as general heaven's war was not snuffed out the roots, it manifested upon the earth, causing more fatalities then I can count. I believe my being here is for the sole purpose of protecting you.

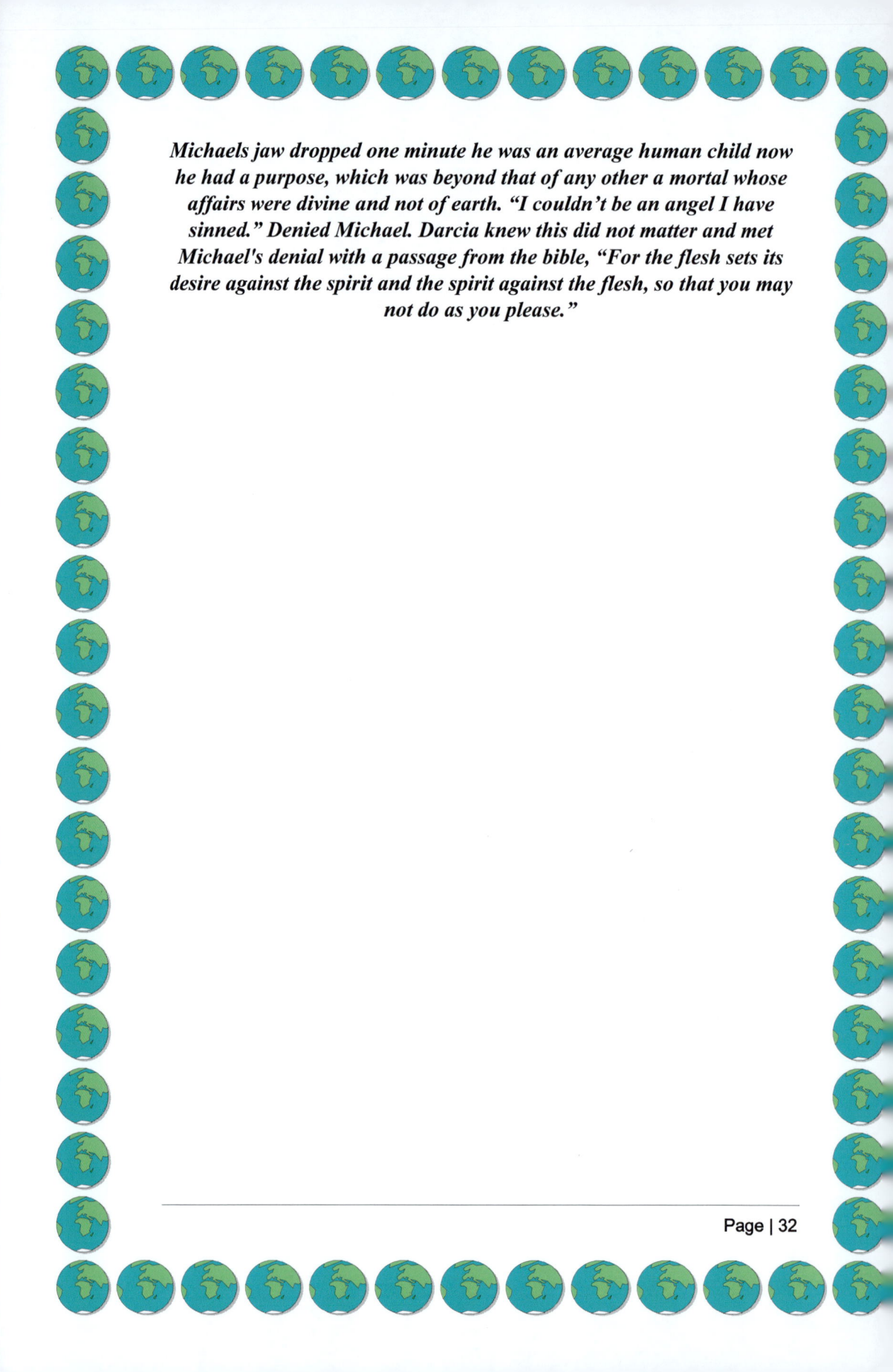

Michaels jaw dropped one minute he was an average human child now he had a purpose, which was beyond that of any other a mortal whose affairs were divine and not of earth. "I couldn't be an angel I have sinned." Denied Michael. Darcia knew this did not matter and met Michael's denial with a passage from the bible, "For the flesh sets its desire against the spirit and the spirit against the flesh, so that you may not do as you please."

Chapter 6 a mother possessed

For a few moments, Michael pondered upon these words to make sense of it in his head; he did not understand how he was so special. Still, he kind of thought it could not be real; the verse started to made sense, but that did not mean he was an angel. He understood the parable but still had a question: "does that mean even though my spirit is of a heavenly origin, the flaws of flesh oppose the angelic essence." The words he spoke were wise beyond his years.

"you are an angel. And shall be overcome your trials. Thus, subjugating a sin There is no way sin can subdue an archangel. you are not of this earth, and God would have given you a purpose something to fight for, thus purging humanity of wickedness that has latched itself onto the human heart."

Michael had no clue what about the part that he was supposed to play in the purging of the darkness. He started to worry about earthly things like his mother. Moreover, his age played upon his mind Michael did not want to leave his mother behind feeling blue, because she had lost her only child. He thought becoming an angel would mean his earthly body would die; he knew his mother would not be able to take cope with that loss. Death had already taken to much from her

When his father died, her mental health deteriorated spiralling out of control, and she was prescribed medicine for her depression. She would not get out of bed and frequently cried, which made him cry; he could not bear seeing the woman who raised him in pain. He yelled, "I am too young to go to heaven, it will make mummy sad. she told me I am the man of the house, and I have to take care of her." Tears welled from his eyes, thinking about the terrible state his father's death left her in.

Darcia took his hand and wiped Michael's face; there was a lot of sadness in his eyes and his heart. He missed his father so much but knew he was in a better place he told Michael "your body will remain *alive for the angel resides next to your soul. Allowing the archangel to ascend will stop your mother from suffering, demons want to see you dead and everything sapped from you they will not spare your human soul." This scared Michael the fact that saving this angel did not cause his mother to become a childless widow helped soothe his emotions, and he stopped crying.*

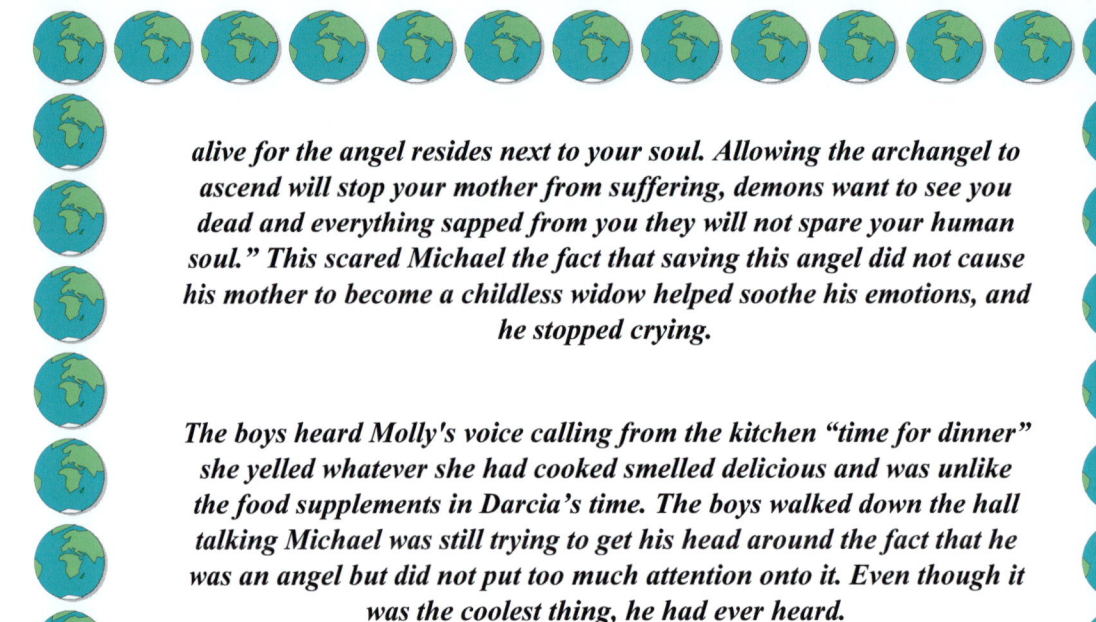

The boys heard Molly's voice calling from the kitchen "time for dinner" she yelled whatever she had cooked smelled delicious and was unlike the food supplements in Darcia's time. The boys walked down the hall talking Michael was still trying to get his head around the fact that he was an angel but did not put too much attention onto it. Even though it was the coolest thing, he had ever heard.

As they reached the kitchen molly's reaction was not at all mother like she lunged towards her son with a sharp knife. Luckily enough Darcia threw him out of harm's way as an automatic reaction. His reactions were on point because of what he had been through in his time. "Why, mummy!" Michael cried in shock.

He never expected his mother to do such a thing she was such a sweet kind lady. She valued life too much; this was not like her at all. This woman was not the same lady that would not even hurt a fly; something was up with his mother. Her breathing was erratic and heavy, her voice rough and rugged.

There was something wicked nested upon her shoulders; Michael's eyes were blind; thus, he was unable to see the demon. Luckily enough Darcia could and shouted, "it is not her fault." To reassure Michael that his mother was not the imminent danger to him, and the evil deed was not hers.

Soldiers like were fitted with apparatus which allowed them to see what the naked eye could not. Darcia started chanting an exorcism in Latin to disperse. "exorciszmus te omnis immundus spiritus omnis satanica protestus, omnis incursio infernalis advasarii omnis legio, omnis congregaio et secta diobolica, ergo draco maledicte ut ecclesiam tuam secura, tibi facias liberatate sevire, te rogmas Audi nos!"

Michael felt a spiritual bond with his mother at this moment the dormant angel awakened from the words Darcia spoke, battles to liberate a soul from otherworldly forces was one of his roles as an angel. Without thinking, he said, "I rebuke thee Satan get behind me."

Then his mother shrieked an awful sound "holy one, you shall taste my wrath." The demon contorted his mother's body in ways that were not humanly possible. Michael put his hand upon his mother's heart and said "be gone, and the holy sword of the spirit spliced the demon from his mother's human soul engulfing the darkness that held his mother's soul for ransom. After Darcia had expelled the demon, Michael's eyes rolled to the back of his head.

Chapter 7 fall of the deceiver

He saw his heavenly origin, the place his angelic essence stemmed from, in a time before his mortal life. His appearance was no longer that of a young boy; he looked older than his earthly human incarnation. His hair was brown, and he had golden pupils, a halo rested upon his head which was so bright it was almost blinding, he had a blue aura and his muscles were gigantic, his wings were silver. They were at their full span pulsating aeronautically high above the vastness of heaven.

The beauty of heaven was beyond comparison, the colour combinations which surrounded him intertwined with a perfect composition it augmented each soul amidst paradise. There was a warmth an overwhelming feeling of love. In the distance, he could see a fabulous bright white light flowing like a waterfall washing over Gods creation. From this light, every soul felt a bliss because Gods love was gushing into every crevice of there being.

He heard a voice which echoed in his ears; it sounded like the first spirit that had merged with him. He felt it calling to him "I am a fragment of memory, remember." Then something flowed into his mind.

It was the beginning of heaven's war; Satan had captured angels who were unwilling to join his rebellion. The concept of his upheaval angered Michael, ever since Lucifer tried to enrol angels during a heavenly assembly to his evil ploy against God, Michael was vext. How dare he try to recruit angels. which fight on the side of God to his wicked scheme., our allegiance is to the creator. "You shall surely fall if you carry out this wicked plot, I beseech you not to take this path." He was angry at Lucifer foolishness, but his words fell upon deaf ears. Lucifer was mad that God would not stroke his ego; he wanted exultation over all of Gods other creations. He believed it earned him a seat at the top because of his works. In response to Michael, he stubbornly roared "I shall make my throne above the stars." Michael reached for his sword; he wanted to cut Lucifer down for his arrogance.

Yet before he unsheathed his sword Gabriel saw what he was about to do and put his hand upon Michael's shoulder as to stop him then pulled Michael to the side, he knew Lucifer was wrong, but there was a code and Gabriel didn't want Michael to break the code. "Why did you stop me have you heard how he speaks against our father," Gabriel answered you know our father very well and know Lucifer shall not succeed his plan. God will thwart his ploy. He is on the road to self-destruction, remember the code father left us. Our we are not to draw our swords against our brethren, Lucifer shall fall by his sword and his actions!"

Gabriel's words calmed Michael down substantially no angel foresaw what happened next some angels slithered on their bellies to join Lucifer's side. Somehow Lucifer found a way to control others. Not every angel in his rebellion joined him freely; he found a way to manipulate their will. This power would one day apply to mortals he would cause many evils and some he would deceive as to make them believe it was the name of God that many would not see god's real face thus they are blinded from falsehoods.

The plummet of many celestial beings into the darkness was how heaven fell, the battle was horrendous heaven was a place of beauty, and war sapped a part of it. Lucifer captured many angels and manipulated their will. So, freeing them was a top priority and Michael's first command, he needed to retrieve every non-disabled angel for the size of the angelic battalion was scarce. Eventually, the number of angels was the right size to put a dent in the enemy forces. Michael ensured the freedom of many angels. He advocated the freeing angels to four of his brethren. Uriel, Hazikiel, Haniel and Zariphel for no-one was to be left behind.

He took the remaining angels into the clash against the demons and fallen angels, who were high in the sky ready for the battle which was about to commence. Michael gave the order for the regiment to fight, but during the war, he noticed Lucifer was not amongst in the skirmish. So, he relinquished his role as the commander to his brother Gabriel.

Gabriel took the reins knowing Lucifer needed to be dealt with now more than ever. He whispered a powerful word into Michael's ears before he left, which would give Michael an advantage over heavens adversary.

Thus, Michael went in search of his brother as to bring the devil to heel; it did not take long to find where Lucifer was hiding for it had a wretched unholy smell. The impurity of the devil had sapped Every ounce of beauty from this part of heaven; it was dark and gloomy. His corruption took root and changed his environment. The most beautiful angel now was so ugly, and he intoxicated everything which surrounded him.

It was not long before Michael reached his brother, whose appearance was warped by bitterness; you no longer could you tell he was an angel; he had become a giant ugly serpent called a dragon. "Repent brother!" Michael yelled which was met by hostility, and the dragon swiped his tail, knocking Michael onto his back.

For a second the monster thought he had won then Michael raised his right hand and uttered the holy words, the beast started to cry because he knew it was over. The words Gabriel had given to Michael was so powerful Satan became afraid. Even though he would have been happier to pull his brother from the darkness, Michael knew this was the only option.

At that moment, a great light came from Michael's hand and wrapped itself around Lucifer and enveloped Michael ebbing from the expanse of Lucifer's hideout. Until it was void and neither Michael nor Lucifer were in that place no more.

The words he used were the same as what filled the holy grenade that Darcia used on Killias. Michael found himself falling through the light, which had overwhelmed his brother. He felt happy that he was able to *purge heaven of such great evil. He heard Lucifer shout in a scornful angry voice "how long shall you be his." And his heart responded forever.*

Soon after he stopped falling, he found himself upon a beautiful field with lilac flowers lay upon the ground, and Uriel took his hand, helping him to his feet. Now is the time brother the battle is not over; you must subdue Lucifer within the world of mortality." Michael knew this time would come and followed Uriel to the tree of life. A place all angels must visit and become a human. As they reached the light his eyes rolled to the back of his head, and he saw a premonition of what was to come, he saw unparalleled pain inflicted upon Gods people, He screamed "that is awful!" then his vision ended.

Chapter 8 A mother's rage

Michaels consciousness returned, as it did a fragment of memory from his life as an angel. When he heard the spirit, it was through a remnant of the connection from the merging in purgatory. Through his newfound memory of his origin, he gained profound knowledge. and spoke from a place of enlightenment "my task on earth is to heal the monsters away."

Darcia had seen hordes of demons, and never thought it was possible for one angelic being to eradicate the masses, he especially did not expect victory over the fends being one move, healing. For he never saw them as an appendage to the earth but as more of a curse. "Like some sort of super exorcism?" Darcia asked as a response Michael nodded his head, reassuring Darcia that his thoughts on the matter were correct.

Then he continued "before my birth; I saw creatures who scared the psyche of God's children. They seemed to be able to enter people's lives undetected, whispering wickedness and sin into people's hearts. They are Influencing humans through every step of their journey, ushering them to walk towards the darkness. People believe their error is by their own choice, but these parasites have a major role, they latch upon the corruptness inside of humanity, and escalate it tenfold. These monsters are so grotesque, and they have a seat within the hearts of the corrupted. If only humankind could see them, the dark forces of sin would not attract them; each bad deed causes a ripple within their souls slowly eroding the beauty that God formed within them."

From Michaels words, Darcia knew this was no small feat. exercising one demon had caused him a whole heap of trouble, so an exorcism that purged masses seemed almost impossible it was hard for him to believe Michael had the power to exercise every last one them in one move. "How is that even possible every demon at the same time?" Darcia questioned. The expression of Michael's face dropped he could not hold a smile because what he was going say saddened him. "The tears of God the Father are the only thing with the power to subjugate demons from this plane of reality. There is a universe hidden from the rest of the cosmos. A place where Gods sadness has manifested itself, a world no angel can bear to look upon for the feelings of the earth are not in the same calibre as this world."

Michael started to breathe erratically; he was panicking because he could not bear the thought of visiting a world where Gods sadness was the dominant force. He found it upsetting to see the pain of humans. So, the idea of witnessing God's anguish hurt him tenfold.

He was unable to finish off his explanation of this place because the panic made him start gasping for air his chest became tight, and he fell to the floor. He had this ailment from the age of five and needed his inhaler.

Darcia started to panic because there was a cure for asthma in his time; thus, it was no longer an ailment. He had seen people pass out but not in the same way as Michael. So, the knowledge of what to do in this situation alluded itself to him. Suddenly a false notion of failure weighed upon him, which made his eyes well with tears.

His wailing caught the attention of Molly, who was in the room next door. Molly was preparing to go for a night out with her friends. She checked up on the boy's she was wearing a sparkling black dress and had pearls around her neck.

She saw Michael upon the floor and dropped down to his level, then checked his breathing. His breath was short, but at least he was breathing his mother loosened his shirt then told Darcia to phone 999. Still, Darcia had another idea the jewel in his hand had matter changing abilities, so maybe he could use that to their advantage healing Michael's health problem. He yelled, "absorb Michael." a beautiful ray of white light, came from the jewel, which was under Darcia's skin. Then its ambience wrapped itself around Michael. The gem was pulling him into Darcia's hand, which glowed with the colour, which represented the archangel, Michael blue.

Molly became engulfed by dread; she had no clue the energy had to come back out. She did not know that Darcia was trying to help.; she was scared for her baby. terrified that her son might be gone forever, she screeched "what have you done with my baby bring him back, bring him back, bring him back!" she frantically swung her arms at Darcia "you monster, bring him back." She was distraught Darcia covered his face; her hits did not cause to much pain because he had felt worse.

He knew her manicness would not stop until she got her son back, so he said "send Michael out well." automatically putting his arm to the side, light poured forth from his hand growing to the size it was when it absorbed Michael then the boy materialised.

Molly was too engulfed by her temper, to notice Darcia had released her son from the miracle jewel. and she was still yelling and swinging her arms "bring him back, bring him back, bring him back." She saw red and wanted to kill Darcia for what he had done to her son, even though she did not understand. She picked up a toy sword and swung it, bashing Darcia until she felt Michael's hand upon her wrist. "Stop mummy; he saved my life."

She turned her head and saw her son with wings regardless of this, she wrapped her arms around Michael and hugged him tightly and asked: "are you, all right honey?" Darcia wanted to know more about the world. Michael spoke of "how do we travel from this world into a world of Gods sadness."

Molly did not understand and from what she witnessed an assumption that Darcia was some sort of a demon entered her mind. The thought of her son's death caused her alarm. She started thinking that whatever Darcia had done caused Michael to enter the afterlife.

This heavenly form was only perceivable by Molly for the angelic side of Michael had touched her soul when Darcia exorcised the demon. She noticed a screwdriver in the hall. And out of irrational fear went to pick it up, but before she could pick it up, Michael uttered, "remember."

Memories of her possession flooded back into her brain she had forgotten about the moment when she was the danger to her son. The memories caused her to fall upon her knees "what have I done, please forgive me." tears formed and rolled down her cheeks. From her memory of the feeling encaged within her own body, unable to control her actions. The feeling of being powerlessness overcame her "what have I done I was helpless I couldn't stop myself; you saved my baby thank you." She sobbed, getting louder with each word.

Michael could not bear seeing his mother in this state, mostly since it was not her fault. He flung his arms around her at that moment she Molly felt the force that set her free and parted the demon from within her flesh. It was so vibrant and beautiful; she became overwhelmed at his presence.

Michael told molly "it is not your fault wicked demons want me dead!" this made her fear for her son "they can't have my baby!" she roared. Michael explained everything that had happened, even his unearthly role. He told her that he was to ascend or at least a part of him and about the time he and Darcia spent in purgatory. She did not want any part of her son to leave his body; she wanted him to remain the same.

Chapter 9 mountain Sanai the arrival of Raphael

Michaels angelic memory of before his asthma attack was foggy, it was like the spirit that conjoined to his own was and had fallen asleep. Truth is Michael's mind had blocked through memories; he did not want to think about a world where Gods was sad. He had to contemplate hard just to get just a fragment, "the mountain," he said, but that was all that came to him, everything afterwards was blank. Then he noticed a tiny horn Darcia had around his neck about as big as a chip and Raphael came to mind.

Raphael was the angel who saved Darcia, the horn around his neck was a gift, that he might call for his angelic aid. Darcia was told upon mount Sanai, to blow the horn three times and the cherubim will hear his call.

Darcia had no clue about how travel worked in this era and asked about portpads Michael's brain became confuzzled "what is a portpad?" he asked. "Portpads create portals which can take you to any destination on earth all you have to do is think it and you are there." Even though the future was catastrophic, there were still elements that Michael found cool. "But where is there this mountain?" Michael asked, not knowing which mountain he saw.

Darcia thought he would have known how to find his brother considering moments ago he was a well of knowledge "Mount Sanai." He said, in an attempt reawaken Michaels dormant memories. Michael knew Sanai was in Egypt, but how on earth were they going to get there. He ran to his room to search for a passport. The realisation that Darcia did not have one came to mind; Michael forgot about the power Darcia which wielded within the palm of his hand. He searched for thirty minutes; whatever Michael was rummaging to find seemed important, so he did not interrupt his search.

When he finally found it, Darcia became puzzled all that time for a little book. Then he opened his piggy bank and counted the money which was not enough to get them both to Egypt. He screamed in grief from the stress, "not enough." "What is not enough?" Darcia asked, "we need the money, and you need a passport." Michael answered, "why did you not just tell me, did you forget what I can do?"

Michael slapped himself in the face knowing he had forgotten about Darcia's ability he also became a little bit annoyed but held it in. told himself It wasn't too big of a deal that Darcia allowed him to search for so long.

Michael gave him a hint as to what he could change; it was his rubbish. So Darcia spoke the words which absorbed matter differently because he wanted it to sound cool "molecules of the rubbish I summon thee." At first, it did not appear to be working. As he was going to open his mouth to rephrase his words, something happened. the rubbish sailed through the air and warped through Darcia's skin into his hand. The only problem that was the jewel did not distinguish what trash was and what Michael wanted to keep even things with sentimental value flowed into Darcia's hand. "No," Michael yelled as a present from his father warped into Darcia's flesh.

Before he could tell Darcia to return the items to their original state, he yelled: "transform to cash." His hand shot money out like a broken ATM; 9 grands must have shot from his hand. Michael had never seen so much money in his life, and he said he said: "wow you could feed the world this power."

The idea made Michael happy and two small feathers poked through the top of his shirt. Neither he nor Darcia realized the key to getting to Sanai involved putting a smile on Michael's face.

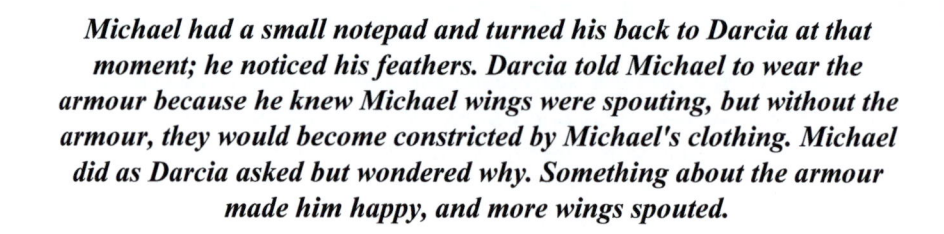

Michael had a small notepad and turned his back to Darcia at that moment; he noticed his feathers. Darcia told Michael to wear the armour because he knew Michael wings were spouting, but without the armour, they would become constricted by Michael's clothing. Michael did as Darcia asked but wondered why. Something about the armour made him happy, and more wings spouted.

He brought the book over to Michael, and it fell to the floor, landing upon a page with art he forgot this cause him to be overwhelmed with happiness. He was glad that Darcia did not absorb this book and suddenly giant angelic wings encompassed Michael's entire back which was the span of his whole body.

He did not even notice them, nor did he feel them as they protruded out of his flesh, at the realization of seeing the transformation of Michael. Darcia guided Michael outside. He put his arms around Michael, thinking he would know to flap his wings, but Michael had no clue he had wings. Until they automatically extended themselves and Michael looked down to see his shadow, which was not that of an earthly child.

At first, he tried to flap his arms, but this didn't work then he looked towards the sky and somehow naturally his wings leapt into flight within less than a second, he was miles above the clouds.

He did not even have to think about controlling them.

"Which way is," his wings sprang into action just before he said Sanai. He did not need the co-ordinates because the angel inside of him knew exactly which way the desired route was to reach the mountain.

The speed of his flight remarkable they were moving so fast neither Darcia nor his eyes could keep up, they were travelling at the speed of light. The colours of everything intermingled into a blur.

In less than a minute they arrived high above Sinai Michael had no clue how to descend. He thought of the ocean and swimming down, and this seemed to work the descent was slower than their ascension.

They landed upon the peak of the mountain, it was scorching, and sand was billowing through the air, the heat caused Michael's mouth to become parched. It felt like being in an oven; it was 43 degrees Celsius.

It was too hot for Michael he was not used to being in the scorching sun because he was from the Uk. he was more used to rain so this heat was a bit much. His skin was unlikely to take to the sunlight well from the fact he was ginger meant his flesh was more susceptible to sunburn than it was to tanning.

When they landed, Michael's wings retracted, and they saw a beautiful woman, whose entire body was blue, including her hair. Which was spikey, and she glowed, her eyes were a fluorescent golden colour, she looked like pure energy. Darcia had never seen such beauty; a pure divine bliss ebbed from her, causing his mouth to open wide. She wore a multi-coloured dress which revealed the side of her stomach and a small part of her shoulder.

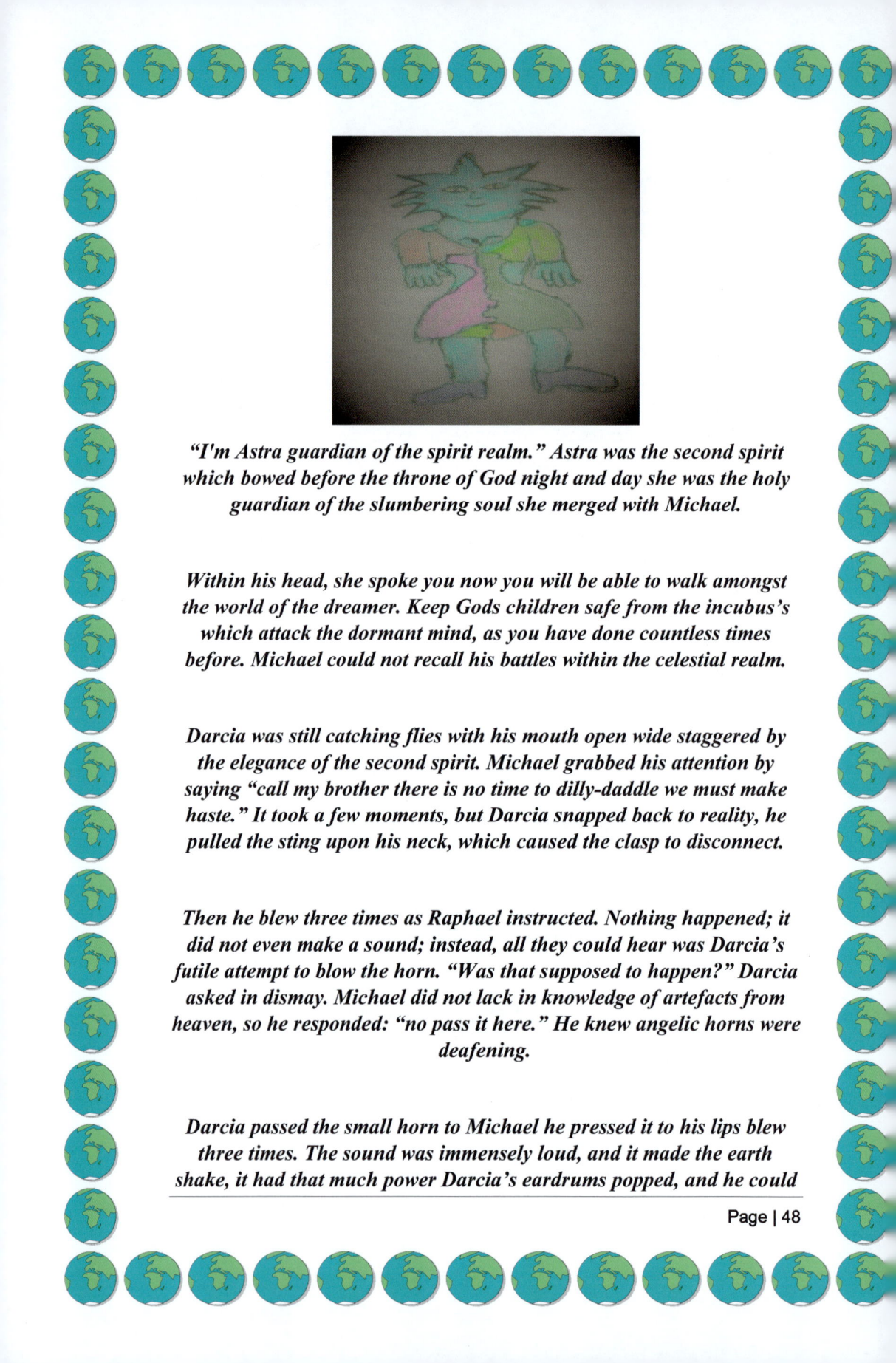

"I'm Astra guardian of the spirit realm." Astra was the second spirit which bowed before the throne of God night and day she was the holy guardian of the slumbering soul she merged with Michael.

Within his head, she spoke you now you will be able to walk amongst the world of the dreamer. Keep Gods children safe from the incubus's which attack the dormant mind, as you have done countless times before. Michael could not recall his battles within the celestial realm.

Darcia was still catching flies with his mouth open wide staggered by the elegance of the second spirit. Michael grabbed his attention by saying "call my brother there is no time to dilly-daddle we must make haste." It took a few moments, but Darcia snapped back to reality, he pulled the sting upon his neck, which caused the clasp to disconnect.

Then he blew three times as Raphael instructed. Nothing happened; it did not even make a sound; instead, all they could hear was Darcia's futile attempt to blow the horn. "Was that supposed to happen?" Darcia asked in dismay. Michael did not lack in knowledge of artefacts from heaven, so he responded: "no pass it here." He knew angelic horns were deafening.

Darcia passed the small horn to Michael he pressed it to his lips blew three times. The sound was immensely loud, and it made the earth shake, it had that much power Darcia's eardrums popped, and he could no longer hear external sounds all he could hear was ringing, everything else had gone silent

The pain Darcia felt was unrivalled by anything he experienced in life; it caused him to fall to the floor. His mind was unable to process anything the horn had caused an unrivalled pain, and He keeled over. Nothing around Darcia mattered he wanted the agony to stop. He was rolling around on the floor he felt like his head was going to explode.

Michael could see Darcia's pain, but as a human, there was nothing he could do for him. Over the horizon, Michael saw his brother majestically flapping his wings heading towards the mountain. It was quite a beautiful and mesmerizing sight, One Michael had forgotten

Chapter 10 a world of Gods sadness

Raphael landed upon the mountain the first thing he took heed of was Darcia writhing in pain, rolling around on the floor. He reached out and touched Darcia ears with the restorative power of divine healing. "The ringing has stopped; thank you," Darcia shouted like as if his ears were still conflicted the raging ringing in his head.

Raphael knew what brought the two boys to mount Sanai. In his possession, he had a vial filled with the grace of six archangels. Then he put the vial to Michael's lips and whispered grace in the Hebrew tongue. A solitude droplet of light fell from Michael's lips into the vial. Within the vial, there was a multi-coloured light which daintily swirled around the vessel.

Grace, in part, was separate through God who knew that in the darkest moments, humankind would face an angel's grace would be likely to liberate and reignite something vital within the human heart. So, God gave the angels a code word that would release a small quantity of grace. If the grace of seven archangels melded as one, the mixture became powerful enough to tear into any other dimension.

Grace itself regenerated from the angelic core faster than blood rejuvenates in humans, the union of heavenly grace, was only forged during situations of dire urgency, and Michael's return to heaven was particularly important.

Raphael poured the content of the vial upon the earth. As soon as the light hit the earth vines sprouted, the vine split down the middle diagonally then grew towards each other until they connected creating a diamond shape. In the centre, there was a translucent thin glass-like substance the vines did not have leaves, but there was an unbosomed *flower at the top which was small and purple and white. Raphael reached out with something in his hand then he spoke. "Take this vial and may the lord walk with you on this journey." Michael took the vial from his brother's clasped hand.*

Then he and Darcia stepped into the translucent portal which was beneath the vines. Neither Michael nor Darcia expected what they saw on the other side of the portal. Within the world of Gods sadness, there was a civilization just like that of the earth, but everything seemed glum. Which caused Michael to become inundated with unhappiness; he felt a heavy weight upon his soul.

This sadness penetrated his mind he could sense God's pain which produced anguish; it was too much for him to stomach. He freaked out his breathing was heavy and lucky for him. The miracle jewel had healed his health condition, or else he may have had another asthma attack.

He felt disheartened knowing this place was a world God sadness manifested and that affected him negatively, but that was the expected result considering he was an angel of the Lord; therefore, he had an extraordinary relationship with God. Within his movement, you could see how the empathic link affected him. It made him feel uneasy, and so he paced backwards and forwards.

Fortunately, enough Darcia was with him to ground him whose link with God was not the same. He was still able to sense something was off in this world, but it did not cause him to get flustered.

Michael started to cry "God's children I feel their pain I feel their suffering." Tears rolled down his face, something inside of Darcia knew what to say. He wiped Michaels tears, saying, "God will wipe away every tear." There was a hint of something heavenly within his voice which calmed Michael down immensely, yet he was still sobbing.

Darcia's words renewed the strength of his will; thus, he was ready to face whatever made God sad. He preceded onwards with Darcia following at his rear suddenly, and a civilization stepped into the fray. Their eye sockets were empty and around them was charred "no God, no God, no God." They hollered night and day; Time seemed to pass so fast.

The appearance which was perceivable was because they had allowed their souls to become blinded by earthly things; furthermore, there was a hollow emptiness within their souls. Then they uttered, "help we're lost, help we're lost." Their cry echoed in Michael's ears and almost caused his gloominess to return, but he knew if he were unable to face this than how could he proceed with his mission.

The souls started to seek some kind acknowledgement of God, "prove it, there is no God prove it." Michael felt a strong urge to admonish these thoughts, but he knew that would not help them to see. "You poor souls God is real; he is right by you, but you don't see." Michaels words were loud and clear; many of these spirits vanished "lost!" they screeched before they disappeared without knowing God.

There was a remnant of hope in some of them. that allowed them to cling to the world. And not perish, like the others. Michael guided them to see the hand that had been there all their lives—renewing their spirits' sight.

Michael setting them free awakened the third spirit hope, which he had helped to rebuild within peoples' souls. Michael had awakened hope which once lay dormant within these people's hearts. Their blindness caused hope to become drowsy, for there was not enough light on his crown. His body and crown had many jewels that lit up for every soul that kindled the hope of God within their hearts, and his face did not bear a smile,

"There is not enough light." He said drearily "once upon a time my crown shined brightly even brighter than the stars. But to many people have let me go and set themselves apart from heavenly hope because of the manacles of earth, no hope is damaging their souls, mend the rift between within the human heart." Then the spirit stepped into Michael's body.

Chapter 11 broken home the first tear

The world shifted around Darcia everything became dark. Michael had vanished so, too did the third spirit; he was not alone; he heard a snarl. The light returned he found himself in a bright white space void of life. Suddenly, a shadow sprang through his line of sight, so he followed it with his eyes. To look upon a deformed ugly creature This monstrosity had black beady eyes, and its face was blobby, and gunk oozed out of its human-like flesh, yet its form was not that of a human.

The creature pelted towards Darcia whose first thought was to draw for his weapon, Michaels voice echoed in Darcia's mind contradicting his first plan of action "no he can be saved." The yelling was louder than anything he had heard in his mind. The timing was impeccable because a second later and Darcia would have skewered the creature. He touched the creature it started to change it shrunk in size and transformed into a young child.

Suddenly this youngster's life flashed before Darcia's eyes his upbringing was awful, his father did terrible things to the boy, and there was an admission of guilt, which he placed upon everyone within his household. The boy's father told him that he was a mistake and a disappointment and worthless. Which led the boy to be unapproving and doubtful of himself, the abuse deeply rooted from a very young age, none of what his father did was ever his fault, and it was upsetting that his father would hurt him in the way he was. His father's tongue was so harmful, and truth be told his parenting skills were the only mistake in that household.

His mother was no help either she gave up through his omission of guilt which got into her head, and she turned to drugs most of the time she was docile, and drugs took her mind from the active conflict inside of her household. Her husband had reduced the mental image of herself *from a loving kind lady to a decrepit horrid hag; he was able to induce these thoughts into her mind. He was never wrong; somebody else was always to blame for his violent tendencies.*

At school, the boy became attached to the wrong crowd of peers he saw something in them that reminded him of his father. The way his dad treated him put him in difficult situations that were likely to get him into trouble. The fact that the bad kids accepted him gave him the delusional idea that he could wriggle his way into his father's good books.

Darcia felt saddened at the ruthless upbringing the child had endured. A small golden orb of light appeared before Darcia, and he heard Michael voice once again "go to the mother and give her this." So, he went to the mother who was unable to see him unable to perceive a world outside of her own.

She was about to inject that wicked needle that had subdued a part of her for well too long before she could Darcia put the light from heaven into her hands. It Glowed brightly then split in two and shot into the woman's heart and mind she felt a renewal of spirit.

Get up, get up, get up your boy needs you. It is not your fault. The voice inside her head was more prominent than it had ever been. She found the strength to reject the drugs and smashed the needle upon the ground.

Then she waltzed towards her husband, and for the first time in his life, he felt small, weak, and defenceless, she shrieked, "get out of my house." The only option in his mind was to put his wife back under his foot, but that wasn't going to work this time for the light had awakened superhuman strength, as he charged the frail woman he saw a look of determination he had never seen before. She had the power to twist his arm behind his back, and he was unable to move. He squirmed to try and get free, but the woman was too strong, the more he struggled, the more constricted his movement became.

The boy arrived back from school to see his mother in her element "it's not our fault. It is yours it has always been your fault we never raised that arm for you." She howled she picked him up like he was a feather and threw him out of the door the boy just opened.

The young man had never felt so proud of his mother, but most of his life, all he saw was the shell of a broken woman. The years went on, and he grew up happy and proud of himself, unlike the way he would have felt had his mother not found the power to deal with that dreadful man he called father.

No more drugs entered his mother's system, and he was grateful to God for fixing the horrors that plagued his life. His mother often told him God renewed the strength. So, he thanked the lord then faded from Darcia sight. The sky released one small droplet and Michael happened to be in the right place to catch it.

Michael congratulated Darcia on a job well done He was smiling Darcia wondered out loud "is that it? are we finished?" deep down he already knew the answer there was no purging the demons could be that easy. Michael objected using a gesture with his head "the vial is only one-third of the content requirement. My memory is still hazy so filling this vial may be the first of many steps."

Chapter 12 break the yolk of oppression

Darcia and Michael preceded onward with a lack of knowledge of the next step, towards filling the vial with God's tears. Even Darcia started to feel a bit dreary something inside of him felt despair from the sadness which was manifest through god's emotions.

They came across an egg; it was massive they felt a compelling urge to touch the egg. There was something about the egg, which enticed the boys. They had a feeling that something was very wrong with the egg. And they could not stop themselves from reaching out as they touched the egg it cracked down the middle.

Gunk slowly covered them; each of the boys tried to pull away, but they found it hard to move they were being pulled into its yolk the orange gunk covered them from head to toe. Yet the yolk had not split. It felt horrible to be in the mixt of the gunge like liquid it got in their eyes and forced them to close they were unable to open them.

Suddenly they were no longer themselves Darcia was a teenage girl she was small chubby. She was carrying books along a hallway, a tall black hair slim girl called Allegra caused her to fall flat on her face, she busted her nose. "Annie's a hippo, Annies's a hippo" she chanted, and another girl said that" did more damage to the floor then it did to Annie."

Sadness welled within the girl, and she started to cry. Blood flowed from her nose. A young boy named Alex helped her up he had a sparkle in his eyes. He pulled out a handkerchief and told her to hold her nose and lean her head backwards to stop the bleeding. He was the first person in that school to show her kindness everyone treated her like she was an animal and all she wanted was to be treated fairly like everyone else.

The boy told her to tell a teacher what had happened, but the last time she got an adult involved, it got them hurt. She informed her mother about her bully, and this did not go over well when her mother confronted the girl's parents. Allegra's mother was the root of her violence; Annie's mum came back battered and bruised. She was threatened not to inform the police, because snitches get stitches.

The next day Annie saw the result of her mother stepping in Allegra's bullying became more physical ever since then, Annie had been scared to allow adults to step in.

So, she declined to let the principle know Annie had been suffering alone for a long time and was happy to have somebody to talk to finally. They went to class and sat in a room full of their peers. They copied the writing on the whiteboard, out of the blue, the girl coughed "pig." Trying to be as inconspicuous as possible. Throughout her life in high school, the bullying would often be because of her weight, and she had heard every variable word for fat. The negative comments harmed her mind. she did not love herself because of other peoples' opinion; she wanted to end it all. The words reverberated around her mind the toxins of other people had made an imprint and left a scar. She felt unable to talk to anyone the poor young lady felt alone and trapped in the torment of the oppressor.

Suddenly, the young boy spoke out, defending her "she's not a pig you're a pig." There was a familiarity in his voice suddenly she felt less alone the unrefined void of bullying caused her to become complacent. Alex being by her side lifted a heavy burden from her chest, the best part was his sister was the toughest girl in their school no girl would mess with her.

He walked her home, and she kissed him then Darcia felt the presence Michael who conjoined to his essence to break the yolk of oppression. They underwent a separation from the bodies of these children. The *young boy backed up the girl throughout the rest of their school life, and finally, she was happy with who she was.*

Both Darcia and Michael saw something putrid the remnant, a creature that causes division and feeds upon hatred. It had many faces each one represented a form of its malice Darcia drew for his sword, but Michael stopped him, love is the only way to thwart him. Michael went over and hugged the monster he had a warmth about him. To warm for the creature to take it screeched then vanished into small speckles of light the boys had broken the yolk oppressor. So too did the yolk that enveloped the boys and another tear fell from the sky, Michael was almost not fast enough to capture it. God's tears had filled the vial two-thirds of the way.

Chapter 13 last tear the almighty appears

The boys were traversing through the world of Gods sadness for round about an hour. When suddenly, they heard wailing children. They followed the noise and came across kids who were in distress. Living on the street with no-one to tend for their needs but themselves, causing them only to own ragged clothing, they looked like they had no sustenance because they had no one to care for them.

Michael asked one of the little ones where their parents were the response; he received was unexpected "our families abandoned us, sir, we are all alone and have no one." Their situation choked Michael up, and a solitude tear dropped from the tear duct within his eyes. Darcia seemed unaffected it was like he was unable to see the children, which left this job on Michael's toes and Michael's toes alone.

The world had been an awful place. To these children, because they need people there who do care, they were not supposed to be alone in the world. Michael asked, "the children why have your parents left you?" some explained it was because they revealed something about themselves that their parents disagreed with their uniqueness was not a fair excuse. Some had been abused and ran away, others had been hurt sexually and had an abortion which their parents hated because of their religion, and some made a mistake they were not old enough to understand.

None of the parents' excuses was a good enough reason to abandon your flesh and blood, to tend for themselves. In a world, they were not ready to face. Many horrible things happened during the children's life on the street, which caused damage to their mental health.

Its angered Michael to see these parents using religion as a crutch and justification to act in such a cruel way. He believed parents were supposed to love their offspring unconditionally. Yet this was not the case for these parents they attached themselves to the wrong things within the word of God because they read it with hate in their heart. They did not subject themselves to the most valuable part of each holy book love. If only they looked more in-depth within the words of God, they would know he did not condone such heinous and cruel actions.

Michael wanted his wings to materialise as to show that somebody still cared; the only reason he was there was to answer the prayers of their hurting hearts. Warmth emanated from him, which drew the children near.

Now that they huddled around him; wings sprouted from his back. Covering every one of them with the love of a true father, one who would be at their side no matter what they faced his love would extend to them regardless of who they were, or what they had done for God was forgiving.

Something about his presence: touched the hearts. Some of the parents and they came in search of their offspring. There was some with a stubborn nature, and still, they rejected to love their children enough to seek them out. Hate had lodged itself within their essence, and it was too deeply rooted for an angel to heal.

So, Michael stuck by them as they grew, thus they knew God was by their side during their suffering. in this world time was so quick, and in what seemed like less than a day the children had grown into adults. Some of which Michaels presence guided them to success.

Then their parents tried to weasel their way back into their lives, but in the same way, that they rejected their children, they too were rejected. Karma bit them hard.

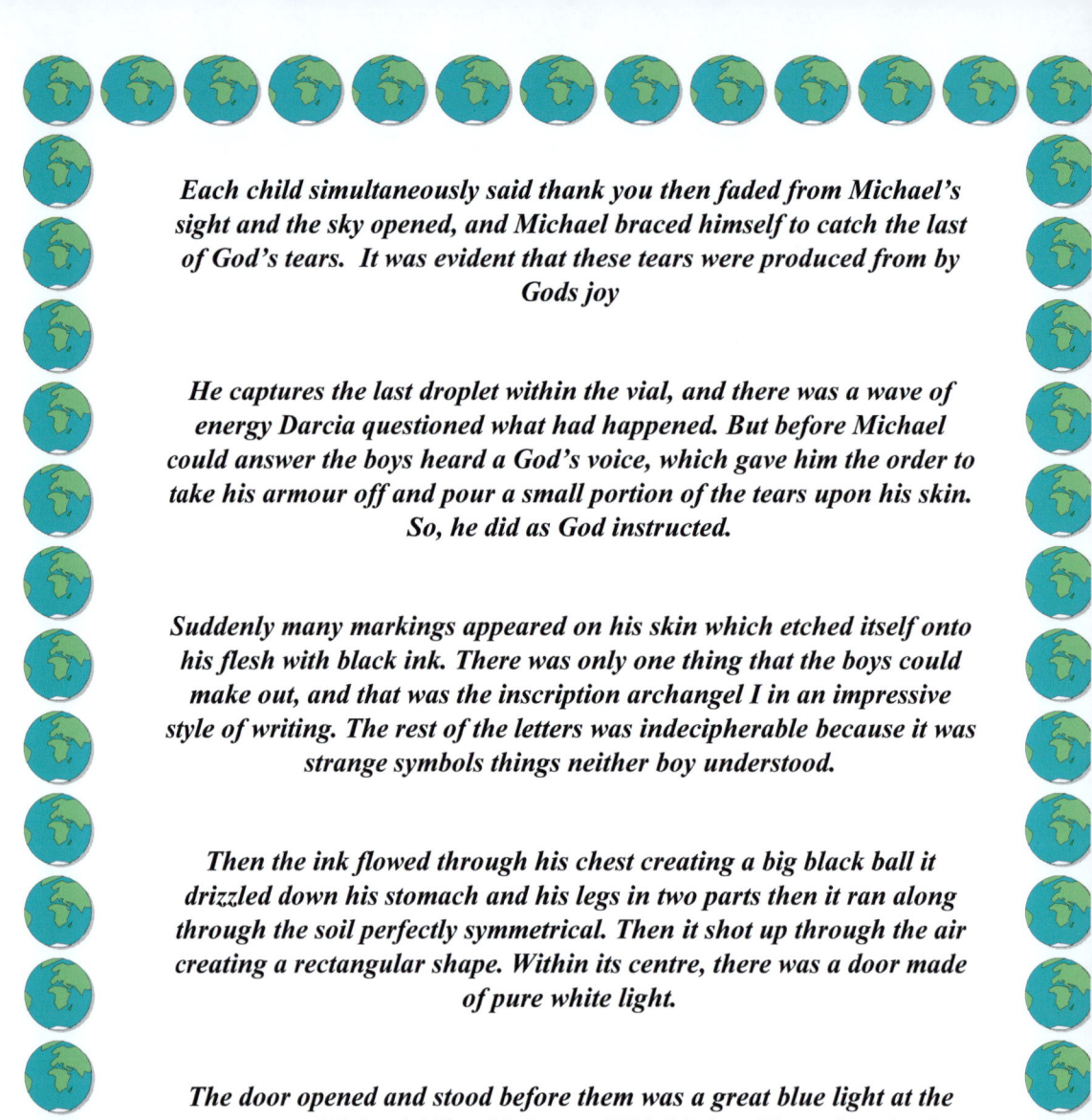

Each child simultaneously said thank you then faded from Michael's sight and the sky opened, and Michael braced himself to catch the last of God's tears. It was evident that these tears were produced from by Gods joy

He captures the last droplet within the vial, and there was a wave of energy Darcia questioned what had happened. But before Michael could answer the boys heard a God's voice, which gave him the order to take his armour off and pour a small portion of the tears upon his skin. So, he did as God instructed.

Suddenly many markings appeared on his skin which etched itself onto his flesh with black ink. There was only one thing that the boys could make out, and that was the inscription archangel I in an impressive style of writing. The rest of the letters was indecipherable because it was strange symbols things neither boy understood.

Then the ink flowed through his chest creating a big black ball it drizzled down his stomach and his legs in two parts then it ran along through the soil perfectly symmetrical. Then it shot up through the air creating a rectangular shape. Within its centre, there was a door made of pure white light.

The door opened and stood before them was a great blue light at the appearance Michael fell to his knees. With his head bowed to glowing being of light. Darcia had not noticed Michael's action, so he never lowered his head. Darcia's did not see the omnipotence of who stood before them so Michael he coughed as a cue for Darcia to follow suit. He realised that this was God; he dropped down to one knee.

The power that emanated from God felt familiar to Darcia, but he did not know why he had never felt such immense power in his entire life. God told the boys to look away, so they did.

A minute or two passed, and the boys got told they could look once again. God had changed his appearance to mimic flesh, but his flesh was not like that of any other persons. It was diverse a mixture of every race rolled into one being this form was his favourite for it showed beauty in all things.

He made it known that the journey to healing the world was not over. Then he clicked his finger, and the boys were back in Michael's room. "weigh the sin." echoed in the boys' ears, but neither of them knew what God meant.

Chapter 14 Flamaldra the sleep paralysis demon

It was late, and the boys felt exhausted; it had been a long and eventful evening. Michael escorted Darcia to the guest bedroom. Which was empty; the only things that were in the room was a bed and a wardrobe. The floor was bare; there was no carpet, and the walls were bare.

Darcia fell on the bed and in seconds the boy nodded off. Usually, Darcia would find it hard to sleep because of the worries there was always fear the next day could be his last. He was afraid demons might attack him during in his slumber. When he was unable to defend, himself but he felt safe here, so he slept with ease.

Michael had to go to the airing cupboard because Darcia did not have a sheet and he knew how cold his house got he took the sheet and tucked him in like a parent would do. Then he headed to his bed and lay down, he tossed and turned for what seemed like an hour. He wanted to get up because he could not sleep, Michael got frustrated with tossing and turning, slumbering was not easy to achieve. Yet, surrender was not an option and eventually, he found himself dozing.

He ended up in a state of sleep known as rem, and he saw his room as it was in his mind. Then he heard Astra's voice "Michael demons have woven themselves into the fabric of Darcia's slumber."

Michael left his room to check on Darcia when he arrived; he heard the boy groaning "No, no." He could not see what Darcia was fighting something, pushed down upon his chest. As he was about to go and try and help Darcia, he was scolded by Astra's voice, "no you can't interact with him, you must find the chalice of foundation it will unweave the loom which subdues his soul."

Michael left the room, but the door led him back to the same destination where Darcia slept. It was like there was in a loop. He tried to leave the place many times, but each time he appeared where he left back the same spot. Being brought back to the same location became annoying, so he thought outside the box and went out of the window. Which led him to another sub-conscience mind that demons restrained.

He left that room, and it felt like he went through 100 doors, but eventually, he came to a world of fire a world a which was a catalyst between those in sleep paralysis and hell itself. A demon induces the conscience brain to have awful dreams who lay beyond the fabric of the mind of those who slumbered.

It was hot sweltering in the distance. Michael heard a voice snarl "the angel I smell an angel." He saw a creature comprised of fire in the expanse, and it was coming towards him, with each step the heat intensified. A memory of this creature's name entered Michael's mind Flamaldra. "Don't let it get to close. Summon the waters of heaven to quench its flames" Michael heard Astra's voice guiding him.

His legs started to dance a familiar dance of their own accord then he spoke in ancient Hebrew tongue. The words he said he did not understand, but it was part of the water dance he was doing.

Above Flamaldra, the sky opened, and rain fell upon it. At first, it did not seem like it affected Flamaldra because the water evaporated from the heat which surrounded Flamaldra. The more Michael danced, the heavier the rain became. rain caused its flames to douse, "this is not over archangel." Flamaldra screeched falling to the floor.

As Michael looked upon the once terrifying flame demon, he saw a scorched carcass of a young boy "help the chalice the boy pleaded. As Michael touched the chalice, he saw a fragment of the boy's life before he became a demon.

His mind became warped by what he believed. he had a bomb connected to his chest for the reward of forty virgins, he was going to hurt a lot of people proclaiming it was in the name of God. He did not see Satan was leading his gullible minds to the slaughter.

No murder was going to warrant the entry into heaven; he did not see the pearly gates. For without knowledge, he had given up his eternity in heaven for everlasting suffering. His suffering would mimic the way he ended many lives. His soul would burn for the rest of his eternity.

The boy was lucky that Michael was an angel and saw he had suffered enough, and his victims were in a better place than himself, he knew the liquid within the chalice could heal his burns but that was no escape there was no way out now.

He closed off the gate to heaven when he murdered a mass of people and died in the process. Being in hell meant there was no way to escape his torture, even if there were no way for him to become Flamaldra again, he would still suffer the consequences of his actions.

He poured a drop onto the boy from the chalice which fell upon him, and he healed his scorched body. Astra spoke to Michael once again telling him he must throw the water on one of the doors. So, he did, and the wickets became dust. Then the dreamers awakened no longer trapped in sleep paralysis by the demon Michael freed them.

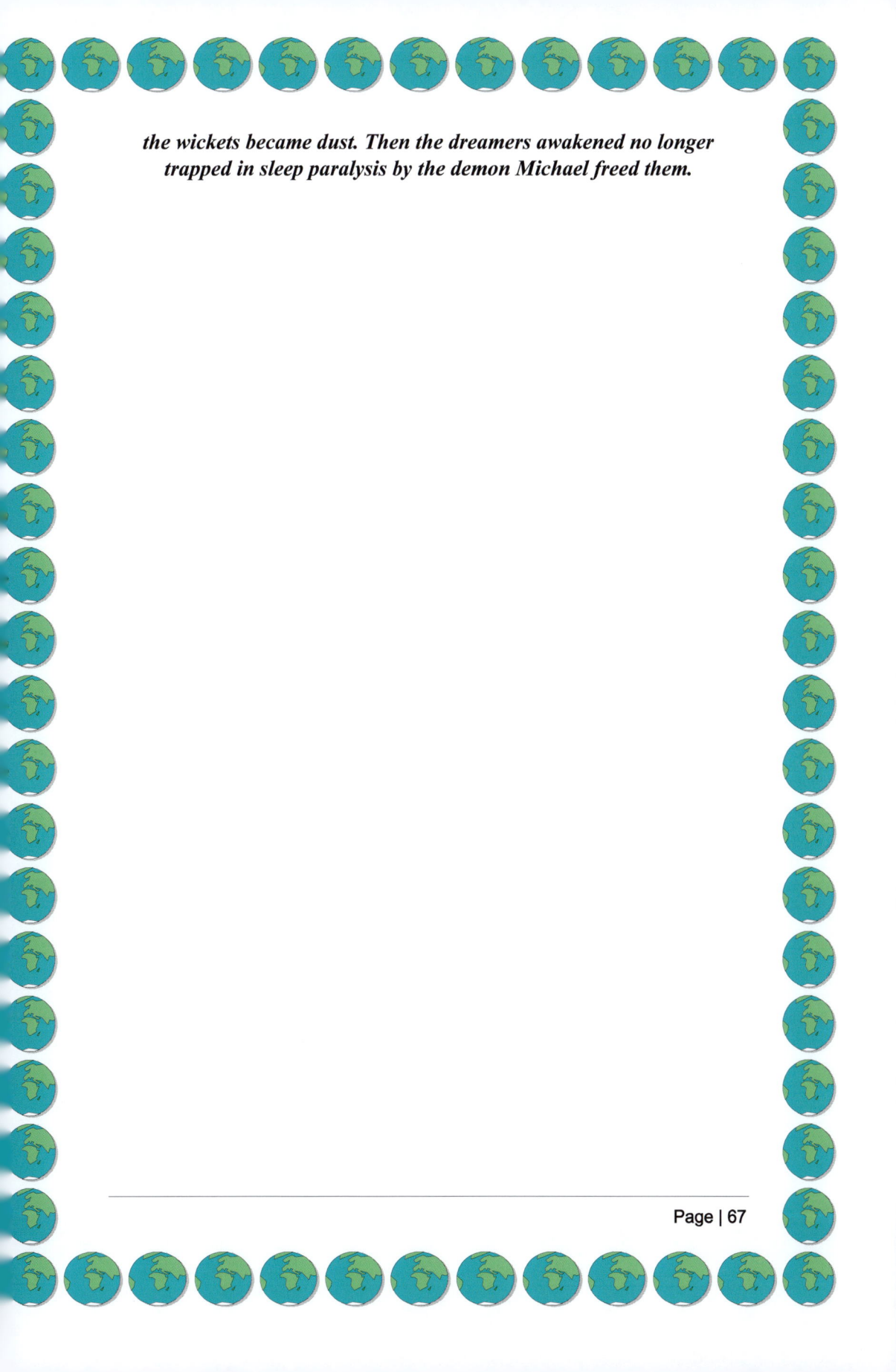

Chapter 15 the prison and the snares

Michael awakened, and his first thought was to check up on Darcia. The sleep paralysis was the first of its kind Darcia had experienced. Where he slept always had warding's so, there was no way for such demons to penetrate his subconscious mind. Weirdly the creature made him doubt himself and his worth. Throughout all his battles, he had never faced a foe that left him powerless unable to defend himself. He had never felt so weak and vulnerable.

As Michael entered the room, Darcia's face was as white as snow. Through the experience in the realm of the unconscious. The night terror washed the Colour washed out of his skin. He was in a state of dread. He could not stop thinking of the decrepit hag that towered over him in his weakest hour. Even though the hag was obliterated by heavenly wings when the dream ended. He still could not get over it.

The sweet smell of pancakes penetrated Michaels' nostril, which made him ecstatic. There was no food he enjoyed more than pancakes with sugar and butter drizzled over them. All he could think about was his pallet, and maybe the food would help Darcia to feel himself again.

Michael renounced the demon, and now he had to find the words to deconstruct the damage it had left. For he could see a part of Darcia was in turmoil from the dream, "What troubles you?" he inquired even though deep down he knew.

Darcia started to explain the pain he had faced and how he had never been in a situation like it. Michael had witnessed night terrors before he became the guardian of slumber. When he had his first-night terror, his mother explained the state of sleep he was in as to quell his fear. She explained the paralysis was nothing more than a reaction in your brain, which stops you from living out the action from your dreams, thus preventing you from getting hurt. So, he explained in the same way his mother had when he first experienced night terrors. He now knew the demons of his sleep paralysis only attacked him because of the vitality of his role to humanity

Breakfast awaited them, and they went downstairs to eat. The boys got three pancakes each. Darcia took a bite without dousing it with sugar, and butter, unlike Michael. "what are these they are gorgeous." Darcia inquired "pancakes" molly conveyed Michael ravished them quickly. It was like the boy did not even chew and asked if there was more. Luckily enough, his mother knew how much he loved them and made an extra batch.

Soon after Michael and Darcia finished their meal, the phone started to ring Michael jumped up excited for, he knew it was his grandpa. His grandpa was a sweet older man, who always looked out for the affairs of Michaels pocket; he did not want to them dry. His grandfather believed young men needed pocket money. Most of the time, he would give him money for nothing, but on the odd occasion, he would ask the boy to do some work to instil hard work reaps the reward.

The fact that he was eighty-two years old meant he found it hard to do what came easy to him in his youth. They had a long conversation, and Darcia could not make heads or tails of it because he was only able to hear half the conversation eventually

Michael asked if his friend could help and his grandfather said yes. Then the call ended.

Suddenly Darcia vanished. Michael sensed something inside of him something long forgotten. He knew he would have to see to the issue to get Darcia back. He sat in meditation to reach the seat of his heart.

Meanwhile, Darcia found himself within a bright red orb which was pulsating around him; the beat almost caused him to fall there were purple tubes which seemed to carry a current.

Within the centre, there was a book floating; somebody had bound the book with chains. Darcia hunted for a key, but all he found was a vial like the one which contained Gods tears. The book called out to him to open its lock with the tears, but as he raised his hand to use the tears, he heard Michael's voice shout "stop!" His voice was just in time to stop Darcia from opening the book.

He turned around to see Michael giving him a disapproving head gesture. Suddenly, a person who was the mirror image of Michael stepped out of the darkness. This doppelganger wanted the opposite of the first incarnation of Michael. "It is the only way this intruder trapped me," he said beguilingly.

This trickster is sealed within Michael's heart and has been for a long time. "the word trapped him well before I knew you it is Lucifer" Michael stated the imposter smirked at Michael with a wicked grin upon his face as if he had already won.

He believed he would have the power to force Darcia's hand. Until he looked in his eye and saw something unwavering and familiar. There was something about the boy he had faced before and lost, but that did not mean he was not going to try his luck

"think of the future I can give you the world you never knew help me" he appealed to what Darcia's wanted, but this mistake caused Darcia denied him. For he had seen false promises sap away the beauty of a human soul. Lucifer wanted freedom and was willing to do whatever it took. Even imposing a lie but his reputation as the king of lies preceded him.

When this did not work, he became angry, and the actual colour of his hatred emanated from his heart. "You dare deny me my throne will ascend above the stars" he could not stand that Michael trapped him within himself. The chains which bound him were chains forged of love, and that made him sick. He did not like being subdued; He did not enjoy seeing the light within Michael's heart.

He feared Michaels ascension for that meant heaven had won, and he would be no more. He knew Darcia's arrival had cut his time in half. He despised Darcia. He wanted to destroy him for it, was through him he would be fade from existence.

There was a time when Lucifer looked up to Michael for, he seemed to be the embodiment of strength. He allowed jealousy to root within him for he felt his brothers received more praise and wanted honour above all things, but God being treated them as equals, but that was not enough for him.

So, he came to Michael with his evil, despicable plan to try and dethrone God, Michael met his words by saying "I rebuke thee" he wanted to cut Lucifer down "you ungrateful." He said as his hand was so close to the unsheathing of his scabbard Gabriel stopped him, reminding him of the angelic code. After which Lucifer managed to subdue a third of heaven. The war began, which in turn led to Michael's incarnation as a human.

Lucifer believed his freedom was looming how hard could it be to make this mortal transgress. He had been able to do it with countless others. In anger, he threatened Darcia "your suffering shall see no end my wrath is kindled against thee" these words sent shivers down Darcia's spine.

Darcia felt the feeling of corruption a dark and vengeful hatred which lingered in the air. Michael yelled, "run it's coming!" Darcia knew this was his only option a warrior knows when it is best to flee. He bolted, knowing whatever was coming was dangerous. As Darcia was running, he heard an awful clicking noise which could only mean one thing a wreath was hunting him.

Wreaths were alpha demons, and their primary function was to sap the faith away from their victim. In the era, Darcia came from he saw many soldiers fall to the power this creature held over humanity. The radius of its power was not small Darcia reached for his sheathed sword, but there was nothing all his artillery was gone. No longer was the boy in the armour which had once protected him and would keep him safe from the scream of the wreath. The first scream was not in his radius; thus, he was safe.

Darcia decided running was the only way he could as to make the distance between him and the wreath. He knew the dance of cherubs was his only chance to survive such an encounter, but the dance required the water from the fountain of the saints.

Darcia came to an open door which led him to a library which meant he was closed off and there was no way to avoid the scream of the wreath. He saw a sign which said fountain of knowledge. He tried to use the miracle jewel to change a shelf into armour, the area he was in nullified the power of the gem.

Suddenly, a book fell in front of Darcia the title was angelic warfare, Darcia heard his pursuer closing in and went to reach for the manuscript. It felt awful he knew the book was the only thing that may give him a chance, but Michaels's voice cut him off "whatever you do, do not open anything you will be playing into his hands."

The wreath popped its head around the corner; it was a shadow like a woman. As it screamed a shadowy ball surrounded it growing as the scream got louder, purple lightning bolted through the orb. Darcia knew there was no way to escape its radius was going hit him. Michael got in the course of the blast trajectory, subduing it for a second "be strong be faithful be vigilant and true." Then the dark energy engulfed Michael, all Darcia could do was wait for the orb to hit him he was ready and did not panic as it hit.

Chapter 16 twisted memory

Seconds, after shadow orb hit. Darcia, found himself back in the war hell hounds overran his platoon. The only way to survive the brutal onslaught was to retreat. Upon the battlefield, there were many dead and wounded soldiers that barely clung to life. It was a horrific sight there was torn flesh and blood splattered upon the ground the carcasses had an atrocious smell.

The commander spurred the surviving soldiers to the portpad he knew many would not survive this attack, for the beasts were hungry for human flesh.

Hell, hounds had features which differentiated them from the domesticated dog. They had spiky fur red eyes and insanely sharp teeth which were able to cause a wound which was impossible to cauterize. One of the hell hounds was in the way of the garrisons only hope of escape. Its mouth was leaking red plasma from the victims it had consumed.

A while before the battle, the stronghold of the cavalry against the tainted was infiltrated, by a shapeshifter. This creature had taken the place of a scout. Who had been sent on a reconnaissance to retrieve information about an enemy? Shapeshifters took their form by consuming the flesh of the one they wanted as their disguise. Their immune system was able to manipulate the genes within themselves to match that of what they ate.

The intel the shapeshifter gavelled them to the ambush unprepared, for a hellhounds bark which can immobilise their targets. Without the proper previsions, they were unable to prepare themselves for the enemy. Thus, many soldiers fell.

The hell hound's eyes pierced into the platoon's soul, causing a lot of them to lose face. Darcia lunged towards the beast, cutting the creature asunder then it changed into droplets of light.

All of a sudden, the world around him warped and he saw the wreath stood beside his mother, and he looked up and what he saw struck terror in his heart Abraxus loomed over his mother.

He was that terrified young boy encased in the cupboard to keep him safe. "The boy where is the boy give him up, and you shall rule at my side." Snarled the demon suddenly, a rush of despair entered his heart, as he realised his mother could have survived if only, she let the creature take him. "It was my fault she died because of me" he cried "it was my fault; it was my fault." He screamed he felt a hand upon his shoulder and heard Michaels voice. "You are not to blame the demon didn't care about that promise. Suppose she had of given you up to abraxas that memory would have torn her apart. For the rest of her life. Which would have been a fate worse than death."

A door appeared in the cupboard where young Darcia and his brother covert to keep them safe from the demon. He wanted to reach for the knob, but his brother stopped "there is nothing we can do."

So Darcia prayed he wanted to be away from this dreaded moment he could not bear the thought of watching his mother die again.

The wreath appeared, but reality warped a third time. there was at a fountain, and six translucent beings of light were dancing the dance of angels. Darcia knew to beat the wreath seven beings needed to dance, so he danced as well.

Out of the water, a spirit emerged whose body consisted of a heavenly liquid, also known as the water of life, the spirit touched the wreath, and the wreath started shrinking. As what will happen to all who stand against the faithful, suddenly Lucifer's face flashed before Darcia's eyes, and he looked terrified "who are you?" He asked trembling then he vanished.

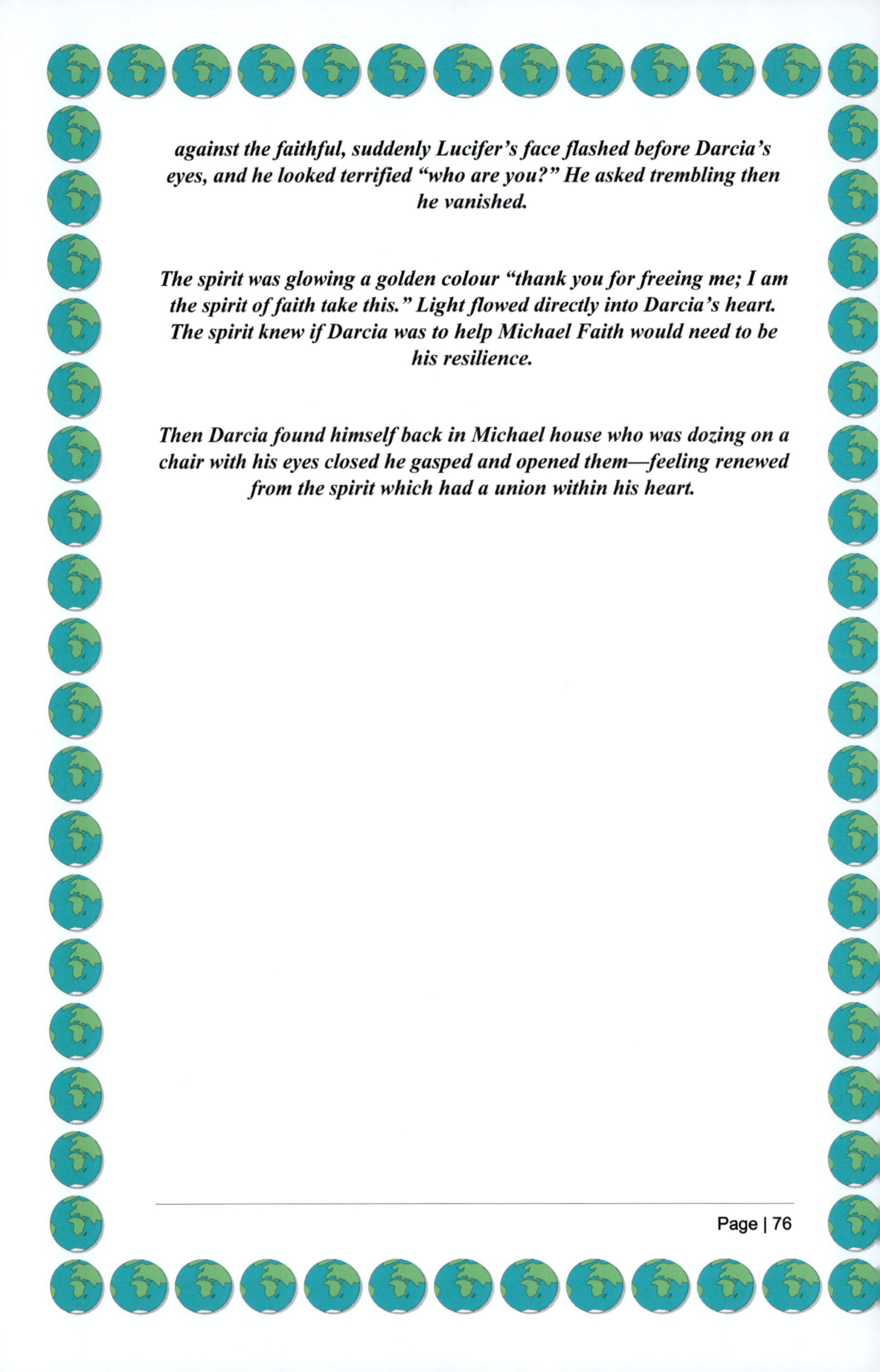

The spirit was glowing a golden colour "thank you for freeing me; I am the spirit of faith take this." Light flowed directly into Darcia's heart. The spirit knew if Darcia was to help Michael Faith would need to be his resilience.

Then Darcia found himself back in Michael house who was dozing on a chair with his eyes closed he gasped and opened them—feeling renewed from the spirit which had a union within his heart.

Chapter 17 poisoned ministry

Michael felt nauseous, and his head was spinning, and he felt a thudding sensation. He had the belief the root cause was the fact that he entered his body from warping through his soul, leaving his brain lacking in oxygen.

Darcia looked upon Michaels face, which was flushed and drawn out. Michael found that he had to compose himself the throbbing in his brain was too much to think straight. During the war, Darcia had seen many soldiers in need of medical provisions, but the medical system worked. Differently, there was not much time to study, so machines determined the health of the world. These machines either sucked illness from your body or replace your antibodies. The device ejected illnesses and would incinerate them.

Michael asked Darcia to retrieve some aspirin from his mother, the system in place in his era made him unknowledgeable about medication such as aspirin. Knowing he was in a different period did not disperse the idea that Michael had to go to the health medic bay. The notions of tablets helping to soothe pain eluded him.

He suggested going to the health med bay, but Frank Linford had not invented it yet. So, Michael gave him a baffled look. He knew the health med bay must have been future tech, inquisitively he probed for answers his curiosity got the best of him. "What exactly is a health med bay" for a second Darcia thought about how to answer, "a health med bay is a machine that stitches up wounds and heals sicknesses."

Michael wondered when machines took over the health profession and what else did machines do that they did not do here and now. Did people lose their livelihoods when machines took over roles ascribed for humans, but he never asked instead he prompted "can you please go and get the aspirin from my mother?"

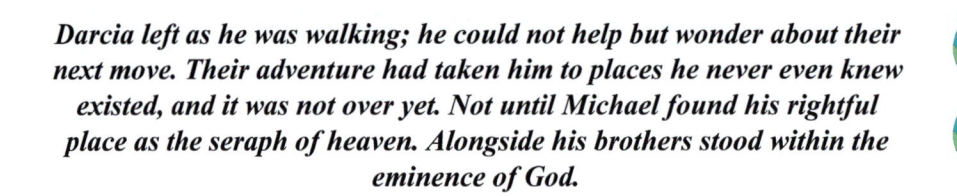

Darcia left as he was walking; he could not help but wonder about their next move. Their adventure had taken him to places he never even knew existed, and it was not over yet. Not until Michael found his rightful place as the seraph of heaven. Alongside his brothers stood within the eminence of God.

He reached the kitchen to see molly standing over a large pot cooking soup which smelt nice. Darcia did not smell good food often because Darcia mostly ate capsulized food; he hardly tasted a good meal. He asked molly where to locate the aspirin she pointed to a cupboard next to the sink Darcia sifted through a medication bag it took a few minutes, but eventually, he found a small tub filled with tablets. He returned to Michael who looked even more ill then he did once before.

He wanted to ask Michael about their next move but was

abruptly interrupted by molly calling them for dinner. The boys went downstairs and as they stepped into the kitchen molly noticed Michaels illness and babied him. After molly did all routine checks to see what ailed him.

Darcia inquired "what is our next move?" Michael put his hand to his chin. He was unsure it was not too long ago that he found out there was a heavenly presence within himself. Michael hardly knew his role as a mortal, let alone an archangel. Darcia saw the uncertainty, and this made him uneasy, he expected Michael to see all roads which led to his ascension. Michael was clueless, but his faith was unwavering.

he responded. "At the moment there is a void within my mind but give it time God is a mysterious God." his words were far beyond his years, and of late he had been surprised at his vocabulary considering he was in the lowest set in English. Darcia's uneasiness faded at Michael's words. After Michael cleaned his plate, he became exhausted and went straight to bed getting to sleep was a battle, but eventually, he nodded off.

The next day Michael felt slightly better but still felt unwell, which suggested his theory was off about what caused his ailment. The next few days were uneventful, and the sickness did not indicate that he was getting better. Michael thought his illness might correspond with Gods plan.

It was Sunday which was his favourite day of the week for he was able to reunite with his family through the blood of the lamb. His church felt like a refuge where all people of all creeds could unite, everyone who entered felt welcomed, and it felt like a warm environment no one felt like an outcast. The blood of Christ diminished all fear and guilt of all who entered everyone was treated equally, and no one looked down upon by their brothers.

There was one thing he had overlooked a promise he made at school, and he was looking forward to seeing his ministry. Michael had no clue what was in store for him at the change of venues. Truth is with how events unfolded he had forgotten about his promise.

He brushed his teeth and got himself prepared to go to church he wore a striking black glittering shirt and jeans when he finished getting changed, he looked glamourous. Then he noticed Darcia's apparel he told Darcia to prepare himself for church forgetting Darcia had no clothing to alter his appearance. As Darcia was about to remind him when the doorbell rang automatically, Michael remembered his promise.

The choice of clothing stumped Darcia he tried on some of Michael's clothing, but they looked silly because they over hanged, so he went back to his original apparel. He thought of using the power of the jewel but had more respect for Michael and would not do that to his property, and he knew the future you had to rummage long and hard for stuff to trade, so everything had value.

Meanwhile, Michael reached the door and inquired "who is it?" he may have found out that a warrior nested within his spirit, but he was still relatively young, and instinctively he knew not to open the door to a stranger. "It's Jacob" a familiar voice replied which was rather high-pitched Michael opened the door to be greeted by not only Jacob but a searing pain in his head, and his nausea became worse.

Michael realised it was not by the effect of the breeze that caused his sickness to flare up becoming more painful, something more cynical at play here. Something had latched itself to Jacobs aura which Michael could not see. Whatever it was made Michael's angel radar go crazy, but Michael's human body could not connect the dots, so his body deduced the signal as an illness.

Jacob was the same age as Michael, but he looked younger than he was, his face had not changed much since the boy was eight years old, he was small. He had mud blonde hair and a bowl cut for his hairstyle. His eyes were baby blue, but when the light shined upon them, they changed colour. His ears were small, and he had a cute little button nose, his build was slender.

Jacob walked in without invitation which Michael found that rude; he found himself holding his tongue. For it was not the worst thing in the world. It was not too long until the sermon started Michael did not want to be late. Tardiness aggravated him, and he liked to keep to deadlines.

His role in heaven could be what made him hate being tardy; it would cause a real problem to Gods children if an angel were late, especially if evil wreaked havoc upon their life. He told Jacob he had to see if Darcia was ready.

He ran upstairs to check Darcia's progress getting ready for church. Then the realisation that Darcia had no change of clothing hit him like a ton of bricks. The idea that Darcia had no change of clothing worried him, and it dawned on his mind that there was a likelihood of lateness.

As he reached Darcia what he feared became a reality Darcia had not been able to change his outfit. Michael's panic overtook him which caused him to pace around his room

As he was walking back and forth like a yoyo, an idea entered his mind "Gideon" he thought, speaking it out loud. He can be cosplaying Gideon. The story of Gideon was his favourite story in the bible. It showed with the lord even in the direst situations God's people can triumph.

Frantically he searched his draw to find a sache as to put a finishing touch to Darcia's outfit when he saw it. He wrapped it around Darcia's neck; it dangled like a cape. There was a picture of Gideon standing upon a hill with the number 300 written in bold red writing Gideon had a sizeable grizzly beard, and he looked healthy. There was a glint where the sunlight hit his armour.

After this, Michael walked toward the door telling Darcia to follow him he knew the feedback he would get from Jacob was not going to be positive for it was not the regular clothing to wear to church. His reaction was not too bad. It reminded Darcia of how Michael reacted when he first saw him "Woah, why are you dressed like a knight?" Jacob asked

Darcia was about to answer with the truth, but before he could, Michael stepped in because the facts may have been too much for Jacob "there was a fancy dress contest at our church, and I forgot to tell him we were going to a different church must have slipped my mind sorry Darcia." Michael found it hard to lie, but the truth was to obscure and out of this world for Jacob to comprehend. He told Darcia his suit was dope and knew if Darcia entered the contest, he was bound to win.

Michael knew they did not have much time till the church stared so he opened the door and stepped out, then asked the boys to follow him. They all walked upon the grass, and there was a gentle breeze which carried the smell of flowers. Michael's hair was going in every direction because of the draft. The pain within his head was growing with each step towards the church something was off, and Michael knew it. They entered a park through a small black gate to see children playing on swings and slides and other apparatus designed for children.

The pain in Michael's head became unbearable; it hurt so bad that he felt faint. Michael realised it all had to be something to do with where they were going.

Jacob picked up a stick to start a sword fight, but Michael was not in the mood for that, his brain was in way too much pain to play. He snapped as Jacob yelled "on guard" "can you please be quiet my head hurts." Michel's reluctance to play Jacobs game spoiled the mood.

Eventually, the boys reached the church car park, and Michael's stomach doubled over on itself. He felt like he was going to puke he looked at the church it has a film like a shadow covering it. A rush of pain made Michael almost keel over onto his face, but luckily Darcia noticed and caught him. He held him up for a few seconds until he gained his composure.

Michael felt like something within the church was sapping his energy; he noticed something was missing something especially crucial because it severed the churches connection to God. The separation from the holy heavenly father hurt him as they reached the door Michael and Jacob were able to proceed, but Darcia was stopped and questioned because of his armour. The usher exclaimed, "This is a church not an arena for gladiators."

Luckily enough Darcia had not forgotten Michael's explanation of why he wore the clothing. "Originally we were going to a different church which was holding a fancy-dress competition, and I was going as Gideon," the usher said "wow that is a well-crafted costume go on in"

The boys took their pew, but the preaching was in no way what Michael expected the priest's words were full of bitter hatred the service did not feel warm and loving like his church or even slightly accepting. The priest's voice uplifted hatred toward people who didn't live by his laws, and he seemed to entangled with verses dedicated to his disgust rather than taking the best part from the book that represented God his mercy and love.

His words warped the congregation's mind not to have sympathy for the downtrodden for their existence was a sin, or at least that was how his words sounded. He spoke of their love, and how it was abominable he would not even allow himself to see their suffering, and he did not care.

His words reduced even those who used earthly methods to escape the pain. To no more than a sinner. No one questioned his teachings; they all just agreed and uttered "amen." Michael knew if there was one amongst them that lived outside of the box; these people would not stay and follow God, for there was too much exclusion to keep everyone faithful.

Michael's jaw dropped, at the unapproving congregation of their brethren lives. They had built babel within their hearts, and even though they were sinner, they believe themselves to better than others.

This man was doing more damage than right turning away flock members that the lord would want to save. Something extraordinary, happened Michael's spirit separated itself from his body and no longer was he upon earth he was in a place known as the veil, which was a world between worlds.

Michael laid his eyes upon the minister once again, to see something his mortal flesh was unable to see. The minster was cloaked by a dark grey sinister mist and each time he spoke it extended and split into segments resting upon each believers' ears.

It entered their mind and took root inside all their hearts. Then, Michael, noticed something grotesque above the priest pulling his strings it was a spirit of hate it sunk its claws deep into his heart and its feet were also in each of the persons' essence who heard him speak.

The creature was an ugly green gooey monster, and it blocked the light of God's love from entering the worshiper's hearts. It hid the truth of the stone the builder refused by replacing it with a dark hatred which lurked tainting hearts binding each of them.

At that moment he realised what was missing acceptance he heard a voice "the sickness you feel was because Gods flock have been bound by hatred and bitterness against their brothers. This intoxication is subduing the greatest feeling of all love. break the chains that they may see Gods light in every soul they reject." The spirit which spoke to Michael was the spirit of acceptance; it wanted to open the door to all and not have them be scared by God's people. The spirits job was to convict, so hate within the sermon did not align with spirits goals.

Michael had no clue what he was supposed to do to break the chains that left wholes within loves dominance. Darcia was the only one the words were unable to touch; he had a light around him. The claws of the creature failed to penetrate his light. Michael felt accustomed with Darcia's eminence, and thus he spoke to it he knew Darcia could spread the illumination of love. to the followers, so he told him to "go onto the podium and speak."

Thus, he did walk towards the green sludge monster. The monster did not want him to get up on the stage, so it made the minister speak against Darcia, but because its claws were in their heart, they could not get close. Darcia snatched the microphone out of the priest's hand. He knew the man's words had corrupted the hearts of God's followers

He spoke "God loves you do not have a prejudice against your brother, for like yourself they are lambs, whom God seeks out when they are lost, he shall find them. The church is not a house of the oppressor. But a house where the oppressed can find strength. From the father who loves them, that they may find everlasting life from the blood Christ." With each word, the radius of the light around him expanded, dividing entering each heart, loosening the grip of the demon on the congregation.

The demon became angry and flew towards Darcia who had no clue about the imminent danger, but as it was mid-air, something spectacular happened golden wings sprouted from his back. Dacia noticed the shadow the wings but did not think anything of it. He believed God sent an angel to aid him not knowing the wings came out of his flesh.

Michael jumped back in shock. The question of Darcia identity entered his mind, soon after he remembered an angel, he had only heard of in tales. The oldest of God's angels an angel, whose sole purpose was to protect guardian angels. From the snake of deceit from the garden of Eden, this angel was called the Golden Cherub he subdued the snake which caused the error in Adam and eve, for it wanted angels to transgress.

Yet the Golden Cherub restrained it until the fateful day that one angel started to become jealous, which caused the snake to break free and enter his essence. If no angel were willing to rebel, the snake would not have been able to enter Lucifer's heart. The Golden Cherub was unable to stop its escape, and thus it claimed an angel and his followers. No angel had laid their eyes upon the Golden Cherub and was only spoke of in legends.

The demon tried to turn back because Darcia holiness became too much for it to take, but it was too late divine fire had entered the monster essence it attempted to flee but it exploded. Thus, Love flooded over the church, and each follower felt a warmth within. They felt the embrace of God's strength and renewal, and it felt amazing. Some started speaking in tongues for the holy spirit had been awakened within their souls.

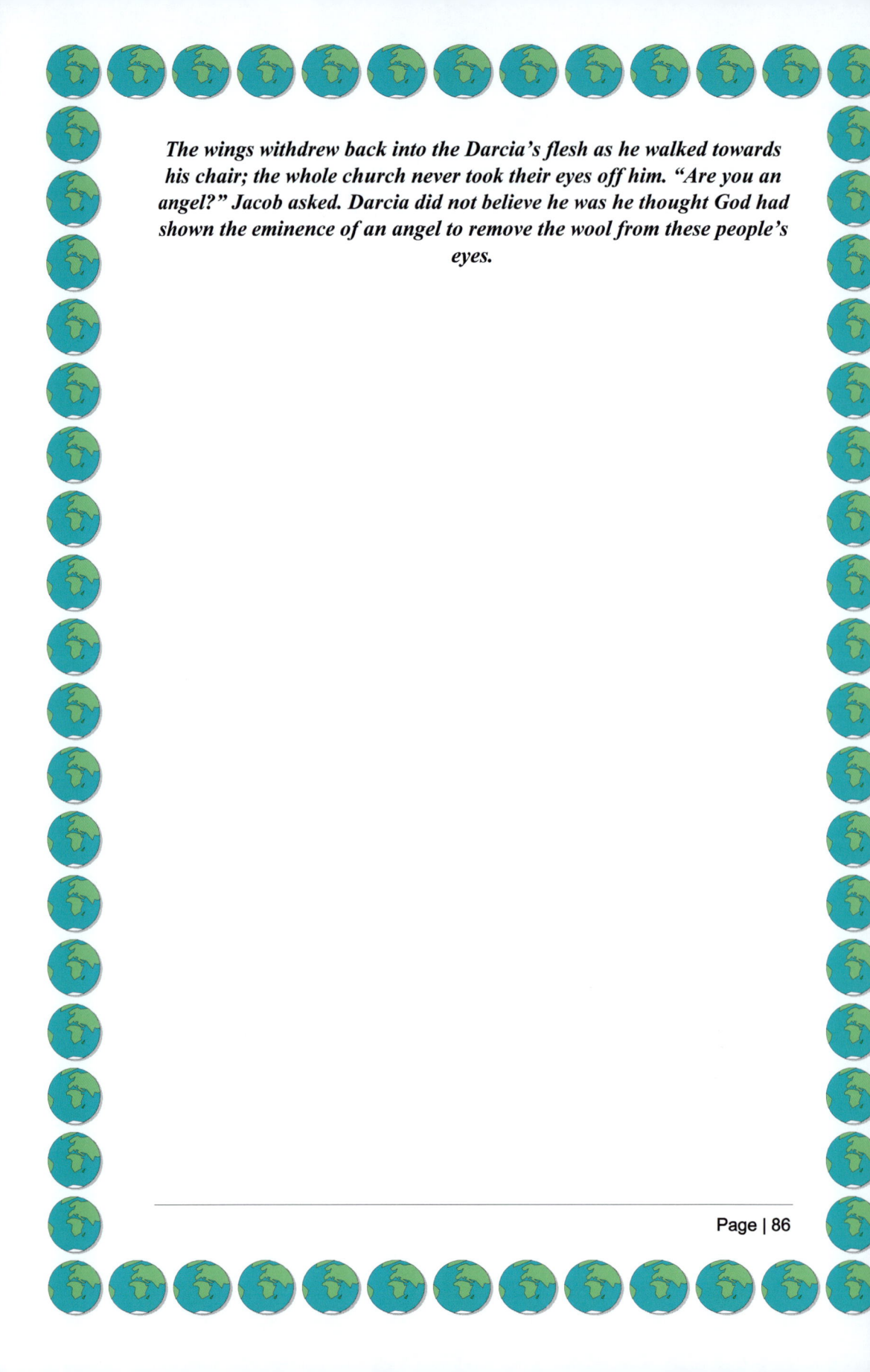

The wings withdrew back into the Darcia's flesh as he walked towards his chair; the whole church never took their eyes off him. "Are you an angel?" Jacob asked. Darcia did not believe he was he thought God had shown the eminence of an angel to remove the wool from these people's eyes.

Chapter 18 the veil and the dragon scales

Michael thought his soul would attune itself back to his body once again, but his body was moving of its own accord. Something else had the wheel, and his head slowly and creepily turned winking at him giving him an evil glare Michael could see the dark intent in his own eyes.

Jacob found it hard to get passed the miracle everyone had witnessed, and he bombarded Darcia with questions. God was mysterious, so the young man did not know how to answer. All he knew was that God had used him to make people's minds unclouded. He was unaware that a skin pirate had taken over Michael's body. Skin pirates were undetectable to Darcia and were able to cloak other dark forces. They were a manifestation which only came to life when darkness took root within the hearts of the faithful sometimes; they were unable to latch themselves fully to the flesh. But with Michael being in the veil, it had an empty vessel. Michael tried to warn Darcia, but his words were unable to travel betwixt worlds.

The creature within his body was a loyal minion to Satan and knew Lucifer's time was short. If Michael were able to heal the world and ascend, the archangel that was within the boy would cure all the parasitic demons out of existence for they were but a scar upon the psyche of humanity.

This demon was part of Lucifer's ploy to escape the destruction he brought upon his head. For that, to work, he would have to gain full control of the body which imprisoned him. He had a plan which would untether him from his prison, which included a scale which he shed upon the earth. He knew Michael could thwart him was able to retrieve the dragon's quill within the veil and wash it in the blood of the lamb before his minion could wash their scale in the fires of hell.

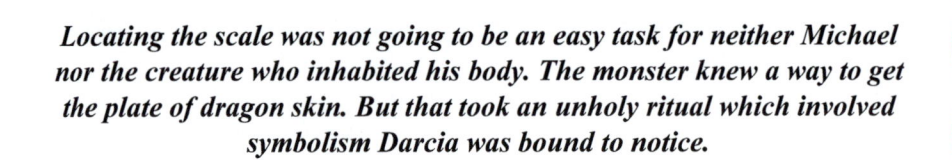

Locating the scale was not going to be an easy task for neither Michael nor the creature who inhabited his body. The monster knew a way to get the plate of dragon skin. But that took an unholy ritual which involved symbolism Darcia was bound to notice.

If its actions were too conspicuous, Darcia was bound to cast it out of Michael's body, and that was not worth the risk, especially after seeing the display of Darcia's cosmic power. With the fact that the mortal body once housed an angel, the demon was unsure it would be able to cause it to follow its will.

Meanwhile, a golden spirit appeared before Michael within the creature's eye's you could see the cosmos. The energy that emerged was the fifth spirit, which sits before the throne of God worshipping day and night. It is the spirit of acceptance. It spoke a husky voice "the earth is in peril. That creature which has snatched your body goes by the name of Eraser. It has one goal, which is to expunge your essence from existence and release Lucifer with no opposition. You must find the scale of the dragon and cleanse it by the blood of the lamb. Find it before Eraser gets its unholy claws upon it.

Michael expected the spirit to merge, but without a physical form, there was no way. The creature spoke once more "the journey will be long and arduous for we must travel to the far through the darkest depths of the veil to reach Lucifer's prison. This world emanates Lucifer and his minions' darkness to the world of men."

Back in the human plane of reality, Eraser hunted for items to initiate his dark ritual. Now that Darcia had cleansed the church the holy light from the faithful people hurt the demon. He found five candles on a tray and blew the fire out as to conserve the string he knew he needed to find a stone.

Eraser felt anxious and uncomfortable because of the presence of the holy spirit; he wanted out luckily for him the service ended. He had to disguise how he felt from being in the presence of Gods anointed because Darcia had freed from the chains which bound them to hatred. He knew it would be suspicious if he showed how uncomfortable he was.

There was an after-church service where the believers could get tea and coffee and a snack. Eraser made an excuse not to participate for he wanted to get out of the church as soon as possible. So, he grumbled, "I don't feel well can we leave." The other two boys nodded, and they left the church.

He knew not to arouse suspicion, or else Darcia would enact an exorcism expelling Eraser back to the veil. He could not let that happen or else he would fail Eraser would compromise Lucifers plan and his very existence

He knew success meant he would have one thousand souls to torture. Eraser wanted Darcia to be one of the souls which he agonised. He wanted him to suffer because he could smell the righteousness of his essence. Eraser hated the fact that the holiness of the holy ghost shrouded the boy. Which Satan nor any of his minions were able to overcome it caused them pain. He wanted to secure Lucifer's victory for then he could have the pick of the crop.

Eraser wanted to flay the love from Darcia's heart, leaving him whimpering in a corner broken with all strength stripped. The thought caused Eraser to break out into hysteria. Darcia became uncomfortable because he never thought Michael laugh would be so sinister. All this made Michael's triumph evermore vital for Gods people

Eraser picked up a stone from off the floor then said: "let us go home." But Jacob told the other two boys to wait for his mother. They did as he asked the only problem was his mother had let him down frequently yet the young man held hope that she wouldn't do it this time, but each time he built up hope in his mother she shattered it.

The abandonment in his time of need made him turn to God for God would never let him down. He needed that consistency in his life; God filled the whole his mother left exposed. He knew Gods love had got him through the darkest times. Even though a demon had clouded his worshipers' minds, he was still able to feel the love of the lord through the shadow. The lord had cleaved himself to the boy's heart as to shelter him with tenderness.

When he first felt the presence of God, he was at his lowest and felt like giving up, if God had not of entered the boy's life would have been 6 foot under because he thought about ending his life. He was a young boy way too young to want to give up.

They waited for hours, and Jacob was in denial that his mother had let him down again Darcia told Jacob to come on, but the boy insisted on waiting five more minutes. Deep down at his core, he knew his mother had let him down once again.

Even though God walked with him, he wanted his mother to be there for him; he needed her physical love. Something in Michael's body sensed the pain Jacob felt, and he wrapped his arms around him, which caused Jacob to feel a loving embrace. Eraser hated the fact that a remnant of Michael's divine love still nested within. Eraser wanted to deny it but did not have that power.

The idea that he did not have full control scared him he wanted Jacob to feel despair and hopelessness. But Michaels body would not allow this then said "God loves you walk with us" this made Jacob leap for joy happiness overwhelmed him. Eraser was shocked how was this vessel able to do that.

So, they started walking back during their journey the sky Became grey, they had waited that long that it had become dark, they could hear the

sound of owls from the trees and crickets in the grass. Eventually, they reached Jacob's house and were about to part ways when Michael body acted of its own accord once again flinging his arms around Jacob. It was as if his body knew Jacob needed to feel love, and Eraser hated the fact he had no power to stop it even though Michael's essence was not their Eraser was powerless to stop this show of affection. He wanted to leave Jacob afflicted by the pain of abandonment. Then Jacob went into his house leaving Darcia and Michael on their travels home.

Torrential rain started to fall which caught the boys off-guard Michael was unprepared usually he would have an umbrella for such cases because the rain was frequent, yet today he had left his brolly behind. By the time the boys reached Michaels house, the rain had drenched Darcia and the husk.

Eraser came up with an excuse to get away from Darcia's presence to enact his plan. He feared the power of the vessel he had taken over he knew it had more power than him and could stop his ritual. He entered the bathroom and investigated the mirror and saw his real face. His skin was black and spikey, and he had three red horns. And his eyes were oozing blood.

Upon the matted floor in front of the toilet, there was a rug. he moved the carpet to be able to draw satanic symbols. He scratched a pentagram

into the wooden floor, and at each corner, he placed a candle. Then he started to speak an ancient evil tongue, asking Beelzebub for guidance every word sounded sinister and twisted you could tell it was a satanic language because it was scary.

Beelzebub was a component of Satan's essence which untethered to his angelic prison within Michael. It was the part of the beast which gave power to all types of fowl principalities which affected humanity. It was a corrupter that no one could see, and the power ascribed to it was to magnify dark intents within the human heart, giving control to demons that they may corrupt the human soul.

Satan never had the power to create so Baalzelebub was formless and had to possess one of Gods creations. Thus, he latched himself to a Goat, becoming Baphomet. Each demon depended upon Baphomet for power and leeched upon the residue Baphomet left behind. His biggest goal was to hurt God, and he knew God's love for mortals was strong, so attacking them and making them turn away would do the trick. God would feel the same pain a parent would feel seeing the one they weened in pain.

Suddenly black line shot to towards the centre outside of the pentagram making a star which resembled the face of Baphomet. A black flame manifested which sucked the light out of the room, just as it had done to the many essences it had touched "speak f f fa" Eraser wanted to call the beast father, but Michaels body would not allow that. A small black flame shot into his Erasers eyes. "We must act fast fa, fa, fa this body will reject your unholy fire." It angered him that he was unable to say father to the serpent of corruption.

Suddenly Erasers consciousness warped out of his body, and he was no longer in Michael's bathroom, he found himself in a room surrounded by cult members. There was a pentagram, and five members were stood around the edges raising a pair of weighing scales. Not what he expected when he heard the scale of a dragon, but it was still a scale. Before he knew it, his consciousness panned to the street, he saw which *road it was on then his consciousness snapped back into Michael's body.*

Meanwhile, in the veil a world which housed demons and all types of fowl things which the world was unable to see. These abominations degraded the human soul as to devalue people in the eyes of God. They Manipulated them from doing all sorts of evils and causing the worst things to root within the human mind, such as hatred, jealousy, and lust.

Before the war in heaven, angels would tend to weed them out as to stop their corruption from manifesting. Demons consumed the souls that fell for their influence. It had been a long time since Michael, or any other angel had supervised the cleansing of the veil. So, the immorality of the nymphs was remarkably high, and they had their claws in many of God's people, and many did not know.

Michael heard an awful screech "they got Hatearger, and he was doing such a great job preparing those juicy Christian souls, that would have been a great feast. If only an angel had not stepped in and rooted his influence with Gods love, we would have a banquet." "An angel! Haven't those fairies been stripped of their wings? I despise those light wielders unless they are under masters control this one is pitiful because its lost has its will." A second voice snarled hatefully

Michael felt a strange sensation there was a familiar presence which he knew from heaven. The angel he sensed was an angel who was the angel of cloaking. Unfortunately, he was the first to succumb to Lucifer's influence Michael's eyes watered for his fallen brethren "Seraquin" he uttered, Seraquin was playful and had a noble heart he made the other angel hearts dance with joy.

Before Michaels tear fell from his face, the golden spirit caught his tear in a vial saying, "we can heal all of them with this." Michael felt joy that his tears could heal his brothers.

In heaven, Seraquin would often use his cloaking to hide he loved to play that game, but the other angels were always able to find him by reminding him of God's love for no angel was able to hide their face from Gods love so Michael uttered: "Yahweh loves you."

The name of the father caused Seraquin cloak to be lowered Michael bolted towards his brother, but the demon cut him off. It was a creature with many heads which was blobby and had goo oozing from its eyes; it had small red spikes with a white root. Each head was the colour of a race. Thus, it had a Caucasian face, a black face, a mixed raced, head an Asian head and an albino head. The separation of the faces was a representation of the division race would cause. The more hatred it could cause, the better the soul would taste, and Satan stalked the earth for souls to consume.

Seraquin retreated because Michael reminded him of what he once was, and that light was too much for him. The creature snapped "never tasted angel" it licked its lips. Its mouth watered with the prospect of a heavenly meal. The creature's mouth rived down the centre like a snake. It plummeted towards Michal as to bite upon his holy essence which didn't work out well the fact that Michael's spirit was 100% pure caused the creature's mouth to bubble after the bite it melted and became a thick pile of Goo—then combusted into ash. The creature's destruction released all the hearts the beast held captive, and the hearts shot towards the people essences which the demon corrupted.

Upon the floor, there was a heavenly sword which must have belonged to Seraquin; he knew angelic swords were able to pierce the Veil which meant he would be able to reach an area of the Veil which was the closest place too heaven. It was the most secure location within the Veil for the most precious part of people was there the hearts of Gods children. Sometimes hearts would vanish because they turned away, and this made angels cry.

Especially when they became irretrievable for the forces which influenced their lives would not allow them to see the glory of the blood of salvation. Michael knew his heart was betwixt the nuclei of all the other people. And thus, he could get to Lucifer's prison.

So he sliced the veil as to get to the well of hearts he stepped into an expanse filled with floating hearts, and at the centre, there was a giant Golden organ with light that flowed to all the smaller hearts. The organ in the centre gave the other's strength; it was the heart of Jesus.

Michael knew he needed guidance to find his heart; Jesus's heart was always there to guide Gods people. A golden ray shot out towards the heart Michael was seeking. Entering the heart was an easy task for an angel, and they would have to do it frequently to uproot sin and bring love and security to the soul that needed it.

So, he touched the heart, and a ray of light surrounded him, and before he knew it, he was in his heart. Using the holy word which he once used to subdue the beast was not an option especially now. Who knew what would happen if he did? The devil had already been imprisoned and uttering; those words could compromise his chances to get the dragon scale.

The fact that Michael was that little bit closer from healing from away the influences of the demons within the veil echoed through the whole of existence. Every monster felt a sharp pain; this caused Eraser panic. He knew he had to act quickly, or else Michael would blot him out of existence.

He did not care too much about Darcia seeing him he knew where he had to god to seal his victory. So, he went outside and transformed knowing Darcia was at his rear green venomous smoke shot from his skin and black, and red wings protruded out of his back he started to flap. Darcia knew there was no time to exercise the demon and never thought about using the power of the jewel. Instead, he reached into his belt and pulled out a small orb and threw it at eraser. The tracker was so close to missing luckily it landed upon Michael's foot, Eraser flapped his wings and shot through the air like a bullet.

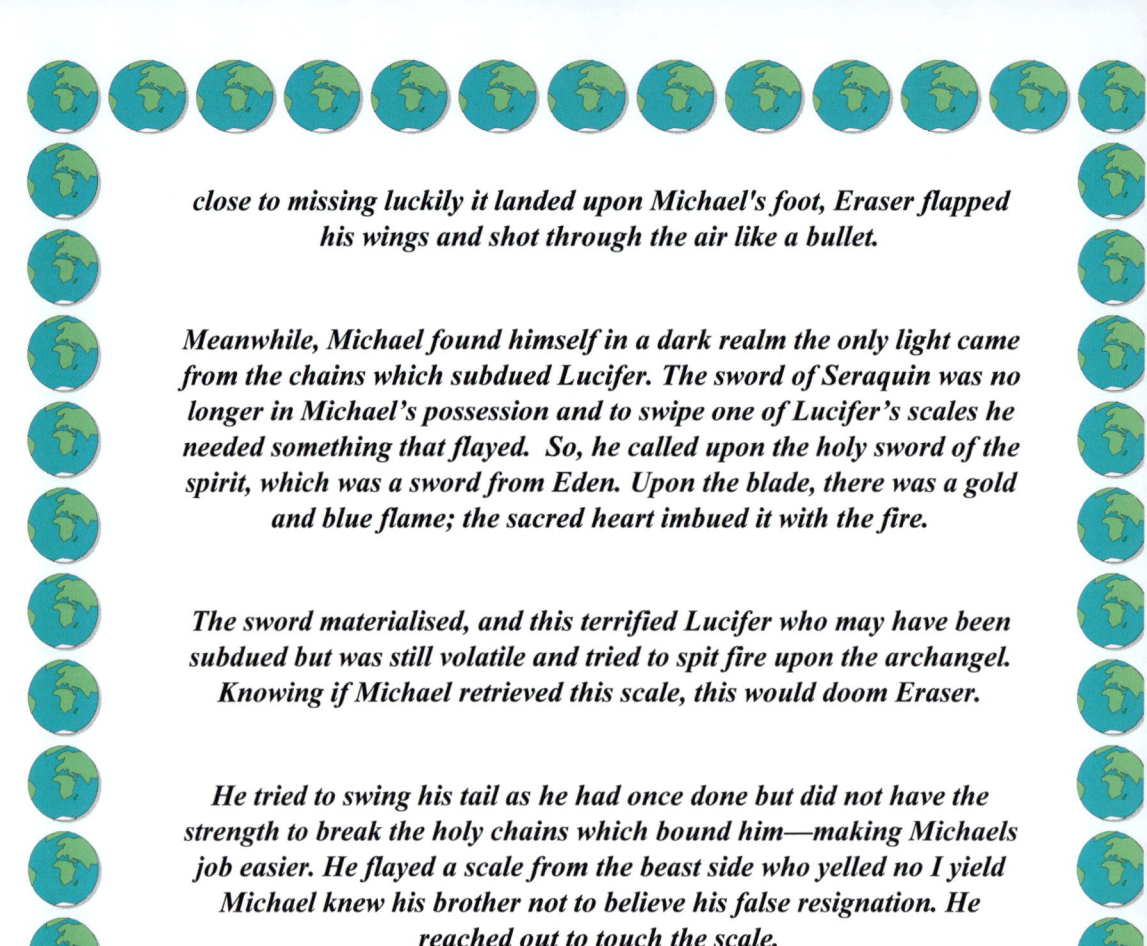

Meanwhile, Michael found himself in a dark realm the only light came from the chains which subdued Lucifer. The sword of Seraquin was no longer in Michael's possession and to swipe one of Lucifer's scales he needed something that flayed. So, he called upon the holy sword of the spirit, which was a sword from Eden. Upon the blade, there was a gold and blue flame; the sacred heart imbued it with the fire.

The sword materialised, and this terrified Lucifer who may have been subdued but was still volatile and tried to spit fire upon the archangel. Knowing if Michael retrieved this scale, this would doom Eraser.

He tried to swing his tail as he had once done but did not have the strength to break the holy chains which bound him—making Michaels job easier. He flayed a scale from the beast side who yelled no I yield Michael knew his brother not to believe his false resignation. He reached out to touch the scale.

Back in the mortal plane of reality, Eraser was getting closer to the scale; he could feel its corruption in the air. Thus, he landed at a shady looking building in the middle of nowhere. There he was greeted by five cult members, and one held up the scale. Both Michael and eraser touched the scale at the same moment this caused Michael's body to go into a trance, and then it teleported into a darkened place within the veil.

Chapter 19 without hand

As soon as the demon left Darcia started to track Michaels body using a radar that was upon his arm after ten minutes the blip vanished. Naturally, his tracker would follow a target but the world where Michael was, no human had ever been. For it was a realm of corruption outside of space and time it was the well of sins.

Meanwhile, the archangel Michaels saw his earthly body entangled in dark roots with his hand clasped tightly around the word sin. he uttered: "let go." Over and over but each time the young man was close to letting and having a victory over sin. Doubt entered his mind; this caused his human hand to fasten around the word tighter. There was no way the archangel going to give up on his host body "let go" he said again, but the corruption was deeply rooted and covered his ears.

so, Michael touched his ear with the sword of the spirit and shouted: "let go." The sixth and seventh spirit appeared conjoined as one repentance with salvation written upon their heads.

Michael knew he had to do something, or else Satan would win. The ghost put its hand upon the boys should calling upon the Golden Cherub, and Michael did the same. The boy's grip was loosening—a wave of energy dispersed through the air as Michael called upon the Golden Cherub.

He would not allow sin to defeat his old vessel; he hollered Golden Cherub two more times; his words were like thunder. It penetrated through dimension's and fell upon the ears of Darcia. Darcia wondered how he could hear Michael.

Then a voice spoke in his mind I have been by your side that I may save Michael waiting for this moment young warrior give me control, and I will end your war. Darcia felt it was the right thing to do, so he gave the

Golden Cherub the reigns. and wings sprouted. Which had a mind of their own, they flapped uncontrollably propelling the bright shiny warrior through the air bursting through the veil which connected each dimension before he knew it, he was at the well of hearts.

He saw one heart which was shrouded in darkness, and something in him knew it was this heart which he needed to tend. The golden heart of Jesus supplied Michaels heart with the strength to deal with the darkness.

Golden Cherub reached out and touching the heart of Michael; darkness had over cumbered his essence. Some of which was dispersed by the divine energy of the Golden Cherub. That was one with Darcia's soul. Thus, his spirit helped take some of the weight from the boy renewing his strength

All the spirits who had united with Michael now stood at his side. Golden Cherub reached his hand through the heart, and it appeared upon the boy's hand. At that moment, the boy heard many voices giving him strength; it was like the whole world was in his corner sin. And from it, he found the power to let go.

There was an awful shriek at that moment the jewel within Darcia's hand dislodged falling through his skin. Its shattered shooting multi-coloured rays throughout the earth every land saw the light. The word sin turned back into the scale of a dragon.

Darcia found himself stood next to Michael, and the weighing scale automatically appeared. Michael picked up the dragon's scale and placed it upon the right side of the weighing scale then he reached into his pocket and removed the jar which contained Gods tears and dripped it upon the scale destroying the influence Satan had on the earth.

Darcia vanished in front of Michael's eyes for the future he came from was no more. He started to weep, "Do not cry, you shall see him soon." a small bit of golden light shot into the boy's heart. Then the seven spirits started to chant "Holy, holy, holy is our God almighty" and they went back to heaven as did the archangel whose mission was complete, he had saved his brothers from Satan's influence.

epilogue

The boy found himself back on earth; he was upset about Darcia's disappearance. The fact that he did not know whether his friend got to see the future he deserved played on his mind. He had made some fantastic memories with Darcia, and something assured him Darcia's life would be alright giving him peace of mind.

The years went by, and he would often think of their adventures and how he could not have saved the archangel Michael without the aid of Darcia. Then one day he had a dream, he was told his wife was about to birth his seed, and Michael named the child Darcia, and he readied him for the lord the heavenly hosts. He knew his child was incredibly important, and even though the child mission left Michael petrified that he would never see him again. He was willing to comply with the will of God.

Meanwhile, from what the boys had done, heaven returned to its former glory. Michael's tears had washed the hearts of the fallen angels from within the veil. Thus, all the angels frolicked. With the joy of God, because their hearts had rekindled, the love they once knew. They danced and praised Gods glory day and night, for he had pulled them from the fire of destruction that Lucifer had wrought.

Angel's still had the task to weed out the corruption within the veil. Dark forces even existed for they were not all forged from Lucifer impurity, some were from the existence of the wicked snake that the Golden Cherub subdued. The snake continued to exist for the balance of the universe

God called upon the archangel Michael for an important task. He told him "it is the time that the Golden Cherub will merge with a mortal. You must subdue the snake in his absence." As Michael accepted the task, his wings became pure gold. Which shined with a blinding light for he had become one with the Golden Cherub. Golden Cherub was the holiest of all the angels.

He found himself next to the holy cherub, and as he turned, it was like Michael was looking into a mirror, the Golden Cherub was him but how. God answered his question "time is non-existent here you are in every moment you shall witness all that the Golden Cherub seen in a moment. Then he took over the battle and subdued the snake until the moment that it found its way into Lucifer.

During that time, the Golden Cherub found his way to the tree of life. Where his journey as Darcia began, he was born, and Michael called him Darcia as God had commanded. Then a thousand cherubs came and took the boy, Michael knew Gods plan was vital, so he did not feel disheartened deep down he knew he would see his boy again.

God commanded Raphael to bring the boy to the alternate timeline and give the child to a woman by a well. So, he did this giving word to the angels in that reality of Darcia's purpose. He even told them of crucial things that made him who he was, so they knew how to play their part.

The years went by, and Darcia did what he could to protect Michael and save the archangel who had been destroyed in his time then the day came when he vanished from Michael's life.

He appeared in front of a great golden light which was God who thanked him for his service and apologised for all he had witnessed. Then he told the boy his true mother and father were waiting for a reunion.

He had confused him for his mother had died in the rebellion, and his mother could not be in this timeline. God clicked his finger, and the boy saw Michael and his mother, who looked the spit of the woman who raised him for she was a descendant of Michael. Tear's welled in his *eyes because he never thought he would see his mother face again. Who was carrying another baby, this is Jarion she said he could not believe he got another chance of a family in time what wasn't catastrophic?*

The years went by, and the new memories Darcia made with his family made him forget all the trauma he had faced. God lifted his pain, allowing the memories of his life in the alternate world to fade, so Darcia felt no more pain. Everything that went wrong was no more God fixed his life. and he lived happily ever after with the family he deserved

The end

Printed in Great Britain
by Amazon